Stilln

The moonlight was so bright that it cast long shadows across the garden. I could see the edge of the black wood. Nothing moved, not even the trees. Everything was still.

Then I looked down at the garden and all the little hairs stood up on the back of my neck.

The nightmare man was standing there.

Other Point paperbacks
you will enjoy:

Ghost Abbey
by Robert Westall

All on a Winter's Day
by Lisa Taylor

Rain Ghost
by Garry Kilworth

Slumber Party
by Christopher Pike

The Babysitter
by R.L. Stine

Party Line
by A. Bates

My Secret Admirer
by Carol Ellis

point

THE NIGHTMARE MAN

TESSA KRAILING

SCHOLASTIC INC.
New York Toronto London Auckland Sydney

ISBN 0-590-43417-9

Text copyright © 1988 by Tessa Krailing. All rights reserved. Published by Scholastic Inc., 730 Broadway, New York, NY 10003, by arrangement with Scholastic Publications, Ltd. POINT is a registered trademark of Scholastic Inc.

12 11 10 9 8 7 6 5 4 3 2 1   1   1 2 3 4 5 6/9

Contents

THE NIGHTMARE MAN

One

Stackfield Pond

I'll never forget the first time I saw the nightmare man. It was one Friday in August when my friend Jay Nimrod said to me, "Let's go down to Stackfield Pond."

"What for?" I asked, surprised. We hadn't been near the pond for months, not since they'd built the new Leisure Centre and we'd spent most of our spare time in the swimming pool. Before that we used to go there quite often, collecting pond life to take to school so's Miss Passmore would give us merit points.

"Birdwatching," Jay said.

I stared at him. "Since when have you been keen on birdwatching?"

He shrugged. "Since now."

Jay's like that. He gets a craze, like yesterday it was swimming, and then he'll suddenly go off it again for no reason in particular. Fact is, I was getting pretty bored with swimming as well. The new pool's brilliant, but once you've swum up and down it a few times there's not a lot else you can do. They won't allow diving.

So I said, "Okay, we'll go birdwatching."

Stackfield Pond's about the nearest thing to real country we've got around Bursley. It lies in waste ground on the outskirts of the town and is shaped like a boomerang, curving around a small wood. As we slid down the bank we could see a few moorhens paddling about and a whole family of ducks, but it wasn't likely there'd be anything spectacular, like a heron or a kingfisher.

"What we need is a vantage point." Jay pointed to where a fallen tree trunk made a bridge across a corner of the pond. "How about there?"

I crawled along the tree trunk until I could look down into the water. "Ugh!" I said. "I'd forgotten how mucky this place is. It's a wonder any pond life can survive."

"Pollution —" Jay was close behind me, "people are always chucking in their rubbish, old bedsteads and cycles and things. I expect it's full of rust." He took off his trainers and socks and sat down to dangle his feet in the water.

"If it's polluted I'm surprised you're putting your feet in it," I said.

He grinned. "My feet are rusty already."

Jay's parents are from the West Indies. He's taller than I am, with long bony arms and legs, which is probably why he's so good at athletics. He holds the hurdles and the 220 metres' record for our school. Normally he wears glasses, but he leaves them off when he's running because they get steamed up. He and I've been friends for about five years now, ever since infant school. We think the same way about most things.

I said, "D'you remember that time we caught an eel?"

"Shut up," said Jay. "We shan't see anything if we talk."

I shut up. In the next few minutes the only bird that came anywhere near us was an ordinary old sparrow, and you can see ordinary old sparrows any day of the week in our back yard. I said, "I think eels are fantastic. They swim here, you know, all the way from Sargasso Sea."

"Alex, I said, 'SHUT UP!'"

More time went by. A chaffinch hopped on to a branch close to where I was sitting and looked at me with his head on one side. Who's watching who? I thought. Jay didn't even notice it.

I said, "I had a nightmare about them once."

"What?"

"Eels — I dreamt I fell into the pond and they twisted themselves round my leg. It was pretty scary."

Jay pulled his feet out of the water. Sitting with his chin resting on his hunched-up knees, he said, "The scariest nightmare I ever had was a huge great brontosaurus chasing me around the school playground. But just as it was about to seize me in its cavernous jaws I woke up."

Not to be outdone I said, "I dreamt once that I was locked in a room with Frankenstein's monster."

"Oh, yeah?" said Jay. "Then how about the time I was stuck in a spaceship that broke down millions of light years away from earth?"

I laughed.

Jay began to pull on his socks. After a minute he said, "Those sort of things aren't really scary, though, are they? They're sort of impossible things.

3

The things that *really* scare people are the ones they daren't even talk about."

He sounded quite serious. I said, "I didn't think anything scared you, Jay?"

"You'd be surprised."

"Go on, then. What?"

"You won't tell anyone?"

"'Course not. What d'you take me for?"

"Okay. The truth is, I'm scared stiff of fire." He stopped pulling on his second sock to stare into the water. "I was in one once, when I was a baby. We were living in a first-floor flat at the time, and someone downstairs threw a lighted match into a wastepaper basket. The stairs caught fire and we had to be rescued through a top-floor window. I was too young to realize what was happening, of course; I only know what Mum's told me since. But I think some part of me must remember, otherwise I wouldn't keep dreaming about it." He polished his glasses with the sock before carrying on. "How about you, Alex?"

"I can't tell you," I said.

"Oh, come on! I've been honest with you. Now it's your turn."

"I don't mean I don't *want* to tell you, it's just that I'm not sure exactly what it is. Sometimes I wake up at night in a cold sweat, as if someone — or something's — been chasing me, but I can never quite remember what it was. Something dark . . . and huge . . . and making a sort of flapping noise." Even just talking about it had made me sweat. I wiped my hands down the side of my jeans.

Jay gave me a curious look. "So you don't know what it looks like?"

I shook my head. The fact is, I'd always had an odd feeling that my nightmare had some connection with

Dad. Or, to be more exact, with Dad's job. He's a policeman, a detective inspector in the Bursley Division, and sometimes he gets some pretty dangerous assignments, yet he never shows the least sign of fear. He just goes out and gets on with what he has to do. What worried me was that I wasn't at all sure I'd react the way he did under pressure. It seemed to me there was a fair chance I might panic and show myself up as a coward.

So I suppose you could say I was afraid of being afraid. The thing that scared me most, haunting my dreams, was fear itself.

I was about to say this to Jay when, suddenly, my eye was caught by a movement on the far side of the pond, and I looked up to see a man standing at the edge of the wood. He was deep in shadow but, as far as I could make out, he was about medium height and wearing a dark suit, like someone at a funeral. I couldn't see his face, it seemed to be hidden by something black, perhaps a darker shadow, but I knew he was looking right at us. There was something odd about him, almost unreal, and for some reason I couldn't possibly explain, it seemed to me he was only there because of what we'd been talking about, as if we'd conjured him up out of our own minds.

Or maybe it was only me who'd conjured him up.

"Jay," I said, "there's someone watching us."

"Where?"

"Over there, by the trees."

He turned his head. "I can't see anyone."

Neither could I. The man had disappeared.

"You're trying to spook me." Jay tied his other shoelace and stood up. "I've had enough for today anyway. It's no use trying to birdwatch without field glasses. Next time we come I'll borrow my Dad's. Ready?"

I jumped up at once and followed him along the tree trunk to the path. I couldn't get away from that place quickly enough.

And that was the first time I saw him — the nightmare man. But it wasn't the last.

Two

The Raven

Dad was late home from work that evening. This was nothing unusual, nor was the way Mum banged the oven door when she took out the plate of chicken and chips she'd kept warm for him. "I'm afraid it's dried up," she said, plonking it down on the kitchen table. "Still, what else can you expect, coming home at this hour?"

She was always in a bad mood when he was late, but I knew — and I think he did too — that it was only because she worried about him. She was pretty tired herself, anyway, after working five hours as a receptionist at the local Medical Centre.

I waited until her back was turned and then said, "Dad . . ."

"Mmmm?"

"Have you ever been scared? Seriously scared, I mean, not just a little bit nervous."

He thought for a moment. "No," he said, slowly, "I don't believe I have — except perhaps once."

"When was that?" I asked.

"Oh, a long time ago. Ten years — just before you were born, Alex. Your mother will know what I'm talking about."

Mum nodded. "The Raven."

"That's right." He sawed off a piece of charred chicken and put it in his mouth.

Puzzled, I said, "You were frightened by a bird?"

"Not a bird." Mum answered for him, because his mouth was full. "The Raven was a man — the worst villain who ever lived in Bursley. Your father was only a detective-sergeant in those days, and he didn't have the experience he has now. He let himself be tricked into following the Raven into an empty house."

"Yes, but I caught him." Dad swallowed the chicken and reached for a glass of water. "I was the one who put him away for ten years."

"Yes, and he put you away too," Mum said, "flat on your back in hospital for six months."

"How?" I asked.

Dad looked grim. "We ended up on a window ledge, just him and me. I told him I knew he'd carried out most of the burglaries in the neighbourhood and he laughed in my face. He said no one would believe me. He was quite a wealthy man, you see, not your usual villain. He even had a seat on the local council. But I knew it was him and I told him I had proof. That's when he stopped laughing and pushed me off the ledge. I fell about twenty feet and damaged my spine."

"Is that when you were scared?" I asked.

"No, it was just before he pushed me, when he swore that one day he'd get even with me. I've never, in all my years in the police force, heard such menace in a man's voice. It turned my blood to ice, I don't mind telling you. I think that's how he managed to catch me off my guard."

"Did he get away?"

"No. By this time there was a reception party waiting for him down below. And it was my evidence that put him inside."

"Which you had to give," Mum reminded him, "from your hospital bed."

"That's right." Dad grinned. "Anyway, his threats proved to be empty, because he never did get even with me. And now he never will."

"Why not?" I asked.

"Because I heard today that he's dead. He died last week in jail. Heart failure, apparently." Dad looked thoughtful. "Strangely enough, I felt quite sad. In some ways I had a sneaking sort of respect for the Raven. He was by far the cleverest villain I've ever encountered."

"Well, it may sound callous, but frankly I'm not sorry he's dead," Mum said. "If nothing else, it means that End House can be sold at last."

"End House?" I repeated. "Is that where the Raven used to live?"

She nodded. "He refused to sell it. That's why it's gone on getting more and more run down and dilapidated all the while he's been in jail. Now perhaps somebody will do it up and make it look respectable again."

I knew End House. It stood in a large, untidy garden at the end of Water Lane, close to Stackfield Pond. And that made me think again about the nightmare man . . .

"Dad!" My sister, Emily, burst into the kitchen, looking rather like a sofa cushion in her quilted red dressing gown. "Mum's so mean, she wouldn't let me stay up till you came home. But I heard your voice. Don't you want those chips?" Without waiting for an answer, she started eating the remains of Dad's supper with her fingers.

"You're nothing but a human dustbin," I told her, pushing all thoughts of the nightmare man to the back of my mind. "No wonder you're so fat."

"I'm not fat," she protested. This was true, up to a point, but she is sort of square, and wears her hair in a straight fringe, which makes her face look square as well. Em's a couple of years younger than I am and full of 'satiable curtiosity', like the elephant's child in the *Just So* stories. She asked, "What were you all talking about?"

"Oh, nothing that would interest you," Mum said, giving Dad a warning look. I don't know why she always tried to stop him talking about crime in front of Emily, because Em loves crime, the gorier the better. She wants to be a policewoman when she grows up. Mum added, "Anyway, you're supposed to be in bed."

"Okay, okay." Emily wiped greasy fingers down the front of her dressing gown. "Dad, will you come up and read me a story? Something really spooky, out of my *Horrors at Midnight* book."

Dad smiled and stood up. "Come on, then." He let Emily drag him from the room.

When they'd gone I said, "Mum, what did the Raven look like?"

"I've no idea, Alex. I never set eyes on him."

She'd answered too quickly, I thought, considering his picture must have been in the local paper at the time. So I tried a different tack. "What was his real name?"

"Arthur Henry Cheyney." The answer came pat off her tongue.

"Why did they call him the Raven?"

"Apparently he had an obsession with birds." She shuddered. "Horrible man. Just thinking about him gives me nightmares."

I was silent. In my mind's eye I could see Stackfield Pond, and the man standing under the trees . . . Could it have been the Raven's ghost I had seen, come back to even up an old score?

But in that case why should he be haunting me and not Dad?

Mum wiped her hands on a towel and came to sit at the table, facing me. She said, "Alex, what made you ask your father if he'd even been scared?"

I shrugged. "Just wondered."

She gave me a long, serious look. "I think you and I suffer from the same problem. We both have too much imagination. It's only people with imagination who can be scared, because they can see the dangers that lie ahead."

"But isn't that a good thing?" I said. "If we couldn't see the dangers we might land ourselves in all sorts of trouble."

"Yes, of course. But ideally we should have just the right amount of imagination; not too much like you and me, — and not too little, like your father and Emily."

I grinned, but I knew what she meant. Mum and I were alike in many ways; both of us skinny, dark eyed and inclined to be moody. Dad and Emily, on the other hand, were solidly built, sandy haired and always even tempered.

I said, "I think Jay has the right amount of imagination. He doesn't get nearly as nervous before

11

a math test as I do."

I didn't tell her about his fear of fire, because that would have been betraying a secret.

She smiled back at me, cheerfully. "Anyway, none of us need worry about the Raven any more. He's out of our lives for good, thank heaven."

Two days later we heard that shortly before his death the Raven had made a will leaving End House, with all its contents, to my father.

Three

End House

"But why?" Mum said, when she first heard the news. "Why on earth should the Raven leave you *anything* in his will, Colin, let alone a house? He was your sworn enemy, for heaven's sake!"

"Maybe he had a guilty conscience," Dad said. "After all, he did put me in hospital for six months. Anyway, let's not worry too much about his motives. The main thing is we'll have a house of our own at last."

"Sell it," said Mum. "And let's take the cash instead."

"Ah," Dad looked a little uncomfortable, "well, I'm afraid we can't do that, Pam. Under the terms of the will, the house is only ours provided we live in it for at least a year; otherwise the entire estate goes to the Royal Society for the Protection of Birds."

Mum stared at him. Then she said, "So, as usual, the Raven has the last laugh."

On Saturday Dad collected the keys to End House

from the solicitor and all four of us went to look at it. At first sight it seemed a pretty gloomy prospect. All the ground-floor windows were boarded up, paint was peeling off the window frames and the garden was a wilderness.

"It's very big," said Emily.

"Too big," said Mum.

Dad pushed open the gate, which was half off its hinges. "Let's go inside."

The front door creaked like something out of a horror film. We stepped into the hall and looked around. It was dark inside because of the boarded-up windows, but there was just enough light for us to see that the place was full of heavy old furniture, festooned in cobwebs.

Dad wiped his finger through the dust on a table. "It's all good stuff," he said. "As you'd expect from the Raven."

"It'll have to go," said Mum. "I couldn't live with any of it."

Emily gripped my arm. "Alex, look!" she breathed. "Look up there."

She was pointing to a dark shape hanging from the wall over the front door. For a moment I couldn't make out what it was. Then I saw that it was a bird — a huge, black bird with its wings outstretched and its beak half open as if waiting to swoop down on whoever came through the door. It was so realistic that for a moment my heart stopped beating.

"It's a raven." Dad laughed. "Trust the old joker to pull a trick like that."

"I think it's brilliant." Emily stared up at it in fascination. "I adore stuffed birds, they're so spooky."

"There's plenty more in here." Mum's voice came

from a room off the hall. "Come and look."

Dad and Emily went to join her. With difficulty, I managed to tear my eyes away from the raven over the door and follow them.

"Ghoulish, aren't they?" Mum pointed to an array of glass cases mounted on the wall containing stuffed owls, pheasants, ducks, even an eagle. "I need hardly tell you they'd have to go as well."

"Come on, Alex." Emily tugged at my sleeve. "Let's look around upstairs."

"Careful!" Mum called after us. "The floorboards may be rotten."

Emily thundered up the stairs ahead of me, two at a time. Once we reached the landing it was much lighter, because the upper windows weren't boarded up. I wondered if perhaps it was only the darkness downstairs that had made it seem so gloomy.

"Isn't it fantastic?" Em was dashing in and out of the bedrooms. "I like this one best, it has a slopey ceiling. Which one do you want, Alex?"

"I don't know yet. Give me a chance."

The first room I entered was long and narrow. I went straight over to the window and looked out. Below me was the back garden, thick with brambles and surrounded by a high wall. Beyond the wall was the wood, and beside the wood was Stackfield Pond.

"I like it here." Emily suddenly appeared beside me, leaning on the windowsill. "There's so much more room than in our old house. And look at that huge garden!"

"Don't get too excited," I warned her. "It's not absolutely settled we're coming to live here yet."

"No, but we will," she said, confidently. "Dad'll talk Mum round, he always does." She gave a contented sigh. "Good old Raven, I don't care if he was a villain. I like him."

"He once pushed Dad off a window ledge," I reminded her.

"Yes, but he was sorry afterwards, wasn't he? Otherwise he wouldn't have left us this house." She pulled my arm. "When I opened the door next to this room I found a little staircase. Where do you think it leads?"

"To the attic, I expect." Suddenly I caught some of her excitement. "Let's go and look."

But before we had time to explore any further Dad and Mum appeared on the landing. "Six bedrooms," Mum was saying. "What on earth do we want with six bedrooms? I tell you Colin, it'll cost a fortune to make this place fit to live in."

"Structurally it's quite sound," said Dad. "And once we've carried out the essential repairs and decorations . . ."

"The rates will be high on a house this size."

"Then we'll take a lodger. There's plenty of room."

"Please, Mum," Emily gazed up at her, earnestly. "Please say we can come. I want to live here more than anything in the world."

Mum sighed. Then she looked across at me. "You're very quiet, Alex. How do you feel about End House?"

I didn't know what to say. I could see that Dad was keen and Emily desperate for us to live here. My own feelings were that End House gave me the creeps, but this was probably because I had too much imagination, as Mum had said the other day. What was I scared of, anyway? A dead burglar? A stuffed bird? A man I'd seen — or thought I'd seen —

standing by Stackfield Pond?

"Well, Alex?" said Dad.

With a shrug I said, "It's okay."

Dad shot a triumphant look at Mum. "Three against one, Pam. You're outvoted." Then he put his arm round her. "You don't really hate it, do you? You said yourself just now that the kitchen had possibilities."

"Yes, it has," she admitted.

"And we'd be mad, wouldn't we, to turn down something that's been offered to us on a plate?"

"I suppose we would."

"So — is it settled then? We take End House?"

Mum nodded.

Emily gave a whoop of delight.

"Provided," Mum said, "that we completely redecorate and throw out every stick of this awful furniture."

"Agreed," Dad said. "Now let's go downstairs and take a look at the garden. I believe there's a summer-house buried somewhere under all those brambles."

He and Emily led the way. Mum put her arm round my shoulders and the two of us followed more slowly. Neither of us said a word.

That night I had my old nightmare again, about being chased by something dark and huge, flapping its wings over my head like some menacing bird. Only now I could put a name to that bird.

It was a raven.

Four

Moving In

Mum only half got her way over the furniture. Dad said some of it was too good to sell and might be useful if we took in a lodger, so for the time being he'd stow it in the attic. Mr Nimrod, Jay's father, came to help him shift the stuff upstairs, while Jay himself gave me a hand redecorating the hall.

It looked better already now that the two high, narrow windows had clear glass in them instead of being boarded up, but the walls were still a sort of faded mud colour. Mum wanted everything brightened up, so Jay and I were covering them with primrose yellow emulsion paint. It was supposed to be non drip, but somehow we'd both managed to splatter ourselves with tiny yellow spots which made us look as if we were suffering from some fatal disease.

"Chinese measles," I told Jay.

"Or a bad attack of custard pox," he suggested.

"Or the dreaded canary-coloured pimple plague."

When Jay had stopped laughing he said, "Talking

of canaries, we'll have to take that bird off the wall before we can go much further."

I looked up at the raven. So far I'd managed to ignore it, although of course I knew it was still hanging over the front door like some threatening bird of prey. The thought of touching it gave me the shivers.

"Do you want me to take it down?" Jay offered.

"No, I'll do it."

I moved the stepladder over to the door and climbed up until I drew level with that murderous beak. Close to, the bird was larger than I expected. Its blue-black coat was covered with a layer of dust, but strangely enough the eyes were still bright. They looked straight into mine with an evil gleam.

"Can you see how it's fixed to the wall?" Jay called, from below.

"There's a couple of hooks, and some wires. I think if I just move this . . ."

Suddenly bells started to ring all over the house. I was so startled I nearly fell off the ladder. Jay shouted something at me but there was so much noise I couldn't hear him. Dad and Mr Nimrod came racing downstairs, Mum and Emily appeared from the kitchen. Then Dad dived into the cupboard under the stairs and, within seconds, the ringing stopped.

"What on earth happened?" Mum demanded.

"Burglar alarm." Dad came out of the cupboard again. "I just switched off the electricity."

"But what made it start?"

I sat down on top of the ladder. "I think it was me," I said. "It happened when I touched the raven."

"Where?" Dad came closer to peer up at me.

19

"Round the back somewhere. I was trying to release the wires."

Dad began to laugh. "The cunning old devil! Imagine — a professional burglar fixing up his own house with a burglar alarm."

Mr Nimrod grinned. "Well, you know what they say, Colin — set a thief to catch a thief."

"But why hasn't it rung before?" Mum asked. "I mean, I can understand that it couldn't go off until the electricity was reconnected, but we've been coming and going a lot since then. Surely it should have gone off every time somebody tried to enter the house?"

"Not necessarily," Dad said. "Alex, come down from there and let me take a look."

When he'd inspected the wiring he said it was a fiendishly clever device, operated by a switch which I must have knocked accidentally. All the wires seemed to run in and out of the raven, which was an integral part of the system. He would have to dismantle the whole thing to put it permanently out of action.

"No," said Mum. "Leave it."

"Leave it?" He looked down at her in surprise.

"This house is very isolated, standing in so much ground at the end of a dark lane. Frankly, I'd feel happier if we kept the burglar alarm."

Dad shrugged. "Okay. I'll just switch it off. Throw me up a duster, Pam. While I'm here I may as well give this bird a springclean."

So the raven stayed where it was and we painted round it. But every time I went in and out of the front door I could have sworn it was looking down at me with its bright, beady, watchful eyes.

Shortly afterwards, we moved in. The garden was

still a wilderness but the house looked quite different once it was filled with our own furniture. At the end of moving day Mum looked round and said, "It's amazing. I can hardly believe this is actually End House."

"It's End House all right." Dad moved some books off an armchair so that he could collapse into it. "Whew, I'm pooped!"

"So are the kids," said Mum. Emily and I were both sprawled on the sofa, clutching mugs of hot chocolate and yawning like mad. "They've worked hard today. Early night for everyone, I think."

For once I didn't argue. Emily grabbed another biscuit — in case she felt hungry in the night, she said — and we both went upstairs. "'Night, Alex," she said as we parted on the landing. "I'm going to sleep like a log."

"So am I."

But as soon as I got to bed I was wide awake again. The problem was that my room felt strange. It was the room I'd come into the first day we visited the house, the long narrow one overlooking the back garden. Now it had been repainted cornflower blue and filled with all my stuff from the old house, but it still felt strange. This is our first night in End House, I kept thinking. I'm actually going to sleep in End House. It was some time before I could bring myself to switch off the bedside lamp.

Then the noises started; odd creaks and groans that seemed to be coming from above me, in the attic. Mum and Dad were still downstairs, so I knew it couldn't be them. I told myself it was probably mice, although it didn't sound like scampering feet, more like someone knocking. I was glad now that Dad had insisted the door next to mine, leading to the attic staircase, should be kept locked. Some of the floor-boards up there were dodgy, he said.

In the end I turned my bedside lamp on again. The noises didn't stop, exactly, but they seemed quieter. Then my door opened and Mum's voice said, "Still awake?"

"Yes . . ." My throat felt so dry the words came out in a kind of croak. "I can hear noises."

"I expect it's the tank upstairs. The hot-water system hasn't been used for a long time, so the pipes are bound to creak a bit at first. Shall I turn your light out?"

"Thanks."

"'Night, Alex."

"'Night, Mum."

After that I didn't mind the noises so much, but I still couldn't sleep. Eventually I got out of bed and went over to the window. I don't know why I did this, except that I had an urge to look again at Stackfield Pond. I didn't need to draw back the curtains because there weren't any: we hadn't got around to putting them up yet.

The moonlight was so bright that it cast long shadows across the garden. I could see Stackfield Pond quite clearly, a sheet of silver water at the edge of the black wood. Nothing moved, not even the trees. Everything was still.

Then I looked down at the garden and all the little hairs stood up on the back of my neck.

The nightmare man was standing there.

His face was in darkness, but turned towards the house, as if he were watching us. I could see his hands, dead white, folded across his chest. My heart was thumping like a hammer, yet I couldn't look away. And the harder I looked, the better I could see

22

him, until gradually his face began to take some kind of shape. Framed by a sort of dark hood, like a monk's cowl, it had a cruel, beak-like nose . . .

I was looking at the face of a bird!

Five

The Lodger

I shot back into bed and buried my head under the quilt. It took ages for the shivering to stop. I didn't dare to look up in case the face appeared outside my window, pecking at the glass with its beak. If only there were curtains, so that I could shut it out! Tomorrow I'd make sure they were put up first thing.

I don't remember falling asleep but, in the end, I must have done because the morning seemed to come quite soon. I got out of bed and went straight over to the window to look out. Of course there was nothing there.

Next day, when Jay came to help me clear the brambles, I told him what I'd seen.

"You must have been dreaming," he said.

"No, I wasn't, honestly. I was as wide awake as I am now."

"And you're sure it's the same person you saw that time near the pond?"

"Yes — well, pretty sure."

I could see that he didn't believe me. He said, "Where was he standing, exactly?"

"Over there, by the wall. It was in shadow, because of the moonlight. That's why I couldn't see his face — at least, not at first." Thinking about it still made me go cold all over, even in broad daylight.

Jay went over to the wall. He stood looking at the spot roughly where I'd seen the nightmare man, near a laurel bush surrounded by tall weeds. "Nothing's been trampled on," he said. "And there aren't any footprints."

"No, well, there wouldn't be," I said, impatiently. "Ghosts don't leave footprints, do they?"

Jay gave me a curious look. "Do you really believe it was the Raven's ghost?"

"What else could it be?"

He shrugged. "Moonlight can play funny tricks. Maybe you just imagined you saw something."

That made me mad. I said, huffily, "I might have known you'd be a septic."

"Sceptic," he corrected. "Septic means something that's gone bad."

"I know what I meant," I snapped.

I turned my back on him and marched off round the front of the house, intending to go and help Dad, who I'd last seen mending the gate. He seemed to have disappeared, but the gate was now back on its hinges and there was a strange man leaning over it.

"'Morning," he said, "Does Inspector Mackay live here?"

"He might do," I said, cautiously. "Who wants him?"

"My name's Tate; Harry Tate. I understand he's looking for a lodger?"

I stared at the stranger. He was short, fairly young

but with light brown hair brushed forward over the top of his head the way men do when they're starting to go bald. His face was very pale and he had a funny little pursed-up mouth that twitched slightly, as if he were amused about something. I said, "How did you know we were looking for a lodger?"

"I overheard someone talking about it."

"Oh, I see." I opened the gate. "You'd better come inside, Mr . . ."

"Tate. Thanks."

I took him through the front door, which Dad had left on the latch while he was working outside, and into the hall. The first thing he did was look up at the raven, but he didn't make any comment, although his lips twitched again as if he wanted to laugh. I said, "If you don't mind waiting here a moment I'll go and find my father."

"No hurry." He took a back copy of the *Police Journal* from the top of a tea chest and started thumbing through it.

I couldn't find Dad anywhere, but Mum and Emily were in the kitchen, unpacking the china and glass. "Watch where you're putting your feet, Alex," Mum warned.

"Where's Dad?" I asked.

"He went into town to buy the screws he needed to fix up some shelves. Why do you want him?"

"There's a man in the hall asking if he can be our lodger. His name's Harry Tate."

She stared at me. "How on earth did he find out?"

"He said he overheard someone talking about it. You'd better come."

She took off the old shirt of Dad's she was wearing to protect herself from the dust and hung it over a chair. As we followed her into the hall, Emily asked me in a hoarse whisper, "Is he nice? How old is he? Where does he come from?"

"Sssh!" I said. "He'll hear you."

Harry Tate was still reading the magazine. As soon as he saw us he put it to one side and turned to Mum. "Mrs Mackay?"

She shook hands with him. "My husband's not here at the moment, I'm afraid. Will you come into the sitting room?"

Emily and I went to follow them, but Mum frowned at us and closed the door. "Oh, pooh!" said Emily. "I wanted to hear what he said." She put her ear to the keyhole.

At that moment, Jay came into the hall. "Alex, I'll have to go home now. I promised Dad I'd . . ."

"Shush!" said Emily. "Can't you see I'm trying to listen?"

Jay grinned. He seemed to have forgotten about our ghost conversation. I went with him to the front gate and we talked for a while, mainly about school. Then he said, "See you tomorrow, mate," and went off down the lane.

I came back into the house to find Emily still with her ear to the door. "They're talking about pigeons," she whispered.

"Pigeons? Don't be daft, Em."

"It's true! He's just asked Mum if it'll be okay if he brings his pigeons. Oh, I do hope he comes to live here! I adore pigeons."

At that point the door opened and Emily jumped back guiltily. Mum gave us both a hard look but Harry Tate was smiling. He looked rather pleased with himself, I thought.

"I'll show you the room," Mum said. "But you do realize I can't make a final decision until you've met my husband?"

"Of course." As he went to follow Mum upstairs he turned around to wink at us.

When they were out of earshot Emily said, "I like him."

"Oh, you like everybody," I said. "You even like the Raven."

Dad came back soon afterwards, just as Mum and Mr Tate were coming downstairs again, and she told him triumphantly, "Colin, we've found ourselves a lodger."

Dad looked a bit taken aback, but he shook hands with Mr Tate, who said he'd like to move in tomorrow if that was all right? Mum said it would suit her fine and Dad said, "Er, well, yes — I don't see why not."

When Mr Tate had gone, Mum exclaimed, "What a piece of luck!"

Dad looked less certain. "Did he say what he did for a living?"

"I gathered he's in show business; some kind of a magician."

Emily gave an excited shriek. "The pigeons! That's why he keeps pigeons — so that he can make them disappear!"

Mum looked at her sharply, but if she realized Emily could only have heard this through the door she didn't comment on it. Instead she said, "I told him he could keep them in the summerhouse once we've got it cleared. Oh, and that's another thing — he said he'd be delighted to help with the garden, if we wanted."

"He sounds too good to be true." Dad frowned. "I hope we haven't been too hasty. Frankly, I'd have preferred to check out his background before coming to a decision."

Mum laughed. "You're a typical policeman, Colin, too cautious by half! I'm a good judge of character, you know I am. Take my word for it, we can trust Mr Tate."

But Dad still didn't look convinced.

Six

The Exact Date

Next morning at school we started a local history project. "We're going to make a scrapbook showing what Bursley was like twenty-five years ago," said Miss Passmore. "Now, can anyone tell me how we set about finding what we need to know?"

Jay put his hand up. "Ask our parents," he suggested.

"Yes, Jay, that's certainly one way of doing it. Any other ideas?"

A girl called Sharon Grimshaw said we could go and look in the graveyard and everyone sniggered. Sharon went scarlet. Miss Passmore gave us all a quelling look and said Sharon was right, we could find out a lot from the church records. "And don't forget our local newspaper," she added. "The *Bursley Gazette* has archive material dating back a hundred years. I've arranged with the editor, Mr Banks, for two of you to go along one afternoon and do some research. Now who'd like to volunteer?"

My hand shot up at once and I nudged Jay in the ribs. Startled, he put up his hand as well and Miss Passmore said we could have the job.

In the playground at break Jay asked, "Why are you so keen to go to the *Gazette* office, Alex? It's going to take us hours to search through all those old newspapers."

"No, it won't," I said. "They're bound to be filed under different years. All we have to do is ask for the copies which were printed ten years ago."

Jay was quick to notice my slip. "You mean twenty-five years ago."

"Oh, yeah — twenty-five."

He gave me a hard look. I tried to appear casual, but inside I was crowing with excitement. What a fantastic opportunity to look up the newspaper reports at the time when the Raven was captured! There was bound to be a picture of him. At last I'd know what he looked like. Not that I expected him to have the face of a bird, of course. But at least it would satisfy my curiosity. All I had to do now was find out the exact date when he'd pushed my father off that ledge . . .

Jay said, "Well, I suppose it'll mean an afternoon away from school, if nothing else. I only hope Miss Passmore doesn't fix it up for Thursday, because then we'd have to miss games. I'd hate to miss games."

I didn't care what we missed. I just hoped it would be soon.

I arrived home that afternoon to find that Harry Tate had already moved in. He hadn't brought much stuff, just what he had with him at the moment, he said. Later he'd hire a van to fetch the rest of his gear, including the pigeons, from his brother's home in South London.

"What made you decide to move to Bursley?" Mum asked, when we sat down to tea. "You'll find it very quiet, especially after London. Nothing much happens here, I'm afraid."

"Oh, I wouldn't say that." His lips twitched.

"I expect you'll be doing lots of magic shows," Emily said. "Making pigeons disappear and things like that?"

"I may do, Emily. The truth is I'm a little out of practice at the moment. I've been semi retired for the past few years."

"You can practise here," she said. "I'll let you saw me in half, if you like."

He laughed. "Thanks for the offer."

Mum poured a cup of tea and handed it to him. "How much gear do you have, exactly?"

"Oh, not too much. Mostly it's props I use for my stage show. I wondered if I could store them in your attic?"

"There might be room," she said. "Although it's rather full of old furniture at the moment, stuff belonging to the man who used to live in this house."

"Ah," said Mr Tate. "I've heard of him, I think. Wasn't his name Charlton or Chepstow or something?"

"Cheyney," I said.

"But they called him the Raven," Emily said. "That's why there's a raven hanging over our front door. He was a burglar." Leaning closer to Mr Tate she added, confidentially, "Once, a long time ago, he tried to murder my father."

"Did he now?" Mr Tate looked impressed.

I could see that Mum was about to shut Emily up,

so I leapt in quickly. "I was wondering, Mum, when did that happen? The exact date, I mean. Do you remember?"

"I could hardly forget!" She gave a short laugh. "As I told you the other day, Alex, it was just before you were born; six hours before, to be precise."

"Six *hours*?" I stared at her.

"It was the shock of hearing about your father. They had to rush me to hospital at once — the same hospital where your father had been taken, only of course I ended up in the maternity ward. You were born at nine o'clock that same morning." She added, apologetically, "But I'm sure Mr Tate doesn't want to hear all these boring domestic details."

"Don't mind me," he said. "You were saying about the attic . . .?"

"Oh, yes — that it's rather full, I'm afraid. But if you don't have too much gear I daresay we could find room for it up there."

"And after tea," said Emily, "we'll help you get the summerhouse ready for when the pigeons arrive. Won't we, Alex?"

"Yes, okay," I said.

So I had my answer. The Raven had been captured on my birthday, 29 January, ten years previously. Now I knew exactly where to look when we went to the newspaper office.

The summerhouse was at the end of the garden, facing south. It was square, with windows on three sides and a verandah in front where you could sit to enjoy the sun. At the moment it was full of cardboard boxes and smelt of mildew, so the first thing we did was open the windows.

"This is perfect," Harry Tate said, looking around him. "The pigeons will love it."

"I can't wait to see them," said Emily. "Shall we start by getting rid of these boxes?"

"No, leave them. I'll do that tomorrow. Let's clear some of the brambles away from the path so that we can get in and out more easily."

While we were working I asked, "Why did you retire from magic, Mr Tate?"

"Call me Harry," he said. "It was due to ill health, Alex. I had to give up for a few years, but I'm okay again now."

"Oh, I see," I said. That would account for his pale complexion, I thought.

Emily said, "You must be glad, Harry, that you can start doing your old tricks again."

His mouth twitched. "Very glad, Emily."

I couldn't help noticing that he was only partly giving us his attention. All the time we were weeding he kept looking towards the summerhouse, as if he'd much rather be clearing away the stuff left inside. In the end I said, "Are you sure you wouldn't like us to give you a hand with those boxes, Harry?"

"Quite sure, Alex. Leave it, will you?"

He'd spoken sharply, and there was a white line round his mouth that suggested he could have a really nasty temper if you got on the wrong side of him. But immediately afterwards he smiled at me again, as if to make up for his snappiness.

All the same, it put me on my guard. I decided maybe Harry Tate wasn't quite the easy going, friendly sort of man he'd first appeared to be.

Seven

Footsteps in the Night

Next day at school we discovered that Miss Passmore had arranged for us to visit the *Gazette* offices on Thursday afternoon. "I knew it!" Jay muttered. "I knew we'd end up going through musty old newspapers when everyone else is out on the football pitch enjoying themselves."

"Oh, stop grumbling," I said. "We can play football any time. You don't often get a chance to look at some real local history."

Jay groaned. "You never used to be such an egghead, Alex. Why are you so keen on local history all of a sudden?"

I muttered something feeble about always being interested, but I knew he didn't believe me. This was probably why, although he went on grumbling about it for the next two days, he didn't try to back out. He was too curious to find out the real reason why I wanted to go.

The first thing we learned, when we arrived at the

Gazette offices, was that there weren't any musty old newspapers. Everything was stored on microfilm.

"We still have the original papers," Mr Banks, the editor, explained, "but they're locked away in a vault and handled as little as possible, in case they get damaged. So you'll have to view them on that screen over there. Mrs Baxter will explain how it works. I'll leave you in her capable hands."

Mrs Baxter was young and pretty and wore very high heels that clacked when she walked. She took a roll of microfilm out of a cupboard and threaded it into the machine, running it through until about half a page of newspaper showed up on the screen. "Twenty-five years ago today," she said, "they were putting up that block of flats in Union Street. That's interesting, because now they're talking about pulling them down again. Nobody wants to live in them. What else would you like to know?"

"Sport," said Jay; "who was in the Bursley first eleven soccer team in those days?"

Mrs Baxter showed us several pages from different editions and we made notes. I kept wondering how I could ask her to change the microfilm without arousing suspicion. After a while I pretended to be more interested in the machine itself than in the information it was giving us. "Supposing you wanted to look up an exact date, say ten years ago," I said, "how would you find it?"

"Give me a date," she said, "and I'll show you."

"How about the day I was born?" I said. "29 January."

"Okay. But we'll have to settle for the nearest Friday, because that's the day the paper comes out." She clacked over to the cupboard again, took out another roll of film and put it in the machine. "Here you are. Do you want the headlines?"

"Yes, please."

Luckily, Jay had wandered off to look at a gigantic street map of Bursley hanging on the wall. I bent closer to the screen to make out the printing. Sure enough, the Raven's capture had been headline news:

LOCAL BUSINESS MAN ARRESTED FOR BURGLARY

And then in smaller capitals:

POLICEMAN INJURED IN WINDOW-LEDGE DRAMA

Disappointingly, the only picture showed a man with a blanket over his head being hustled into a police van. I started to read the report:

Arthur Cheyney, respected member of the Bursley Chamber of Commerce, was arrested earlier this week in dramatic circumstances. While ransacking a house in Dover Avenue he was apprehended by Detective-sergeant Colin Mackay and a violent struggle took place on a first-floor window ledge. During the course of the struggle Sergeant Mackay fell twenty feet to the garden below. A police spokesman said that he had been taken to Bursley General Hospital, where his condition was stated to be satisfactory. Arthur Cheyney was later charged with burglary and resisting arrest . . .

"Good heavens!" Mrs Baxter's voice made me jump. "I remember that incident. It was a terrific shock at the time because my father knew Arthur Cheyney quite well. They often did business together."

I couldn't believe my luck. "Did you ever meet him?" I asked.

"Yes, once. He came to our house one evening to see my father."

"What did he look like?"

"Oh, quite short, balding — just an ordinary businessman. He had an odd sense of humour, though, and was fond of playing practical jokes on people. I suppose that's why he always wore a mask."

"A mask?"

"When carrying out his burglaries, so that he couldn't be recognized."

"What kind of a mask?" Now I was really excited. "A bird mask?"

Mrs Baxter frowned. "I don't remember. It may have been. They called him the Raven, you know."

"I might have guessed!" Jay spoke from right behind us. "So *that's* why you wanted to come, Alex."

Mrs Baxter looked surprised. I felt myself turning red.

"His dad's the policeman who was injured," Jay told Mrs Baxter.

She shot me an anxious look. "Oh dear, I wish I'd known. What happened to your father? Did he recover?"

"Yeah, he's fine," I said carelessly, moving away from the screen. "Thanks, Mrs Baxter. We've got all the information we need now, so we'd better be going."

As we walked back to school — Miss Passmore had made us promise to report to her when we'd finished — Jay said, "I still don't get it, Alex. What were you hoping to find out?"

"I wanted to see what he looked like, that's all." I

couldn't keep my excitement bottled up any longer. "Did you hear what she said? He wore a mask to carry out his burglaries. And not just any old mask either, but a bird mask!"

"She didn't exactly say that. She said it *might* have been a bird mask, she couldn't remember."

"But when I saw him standing in the garden I didn't know he wore a mask. I didn't know that till today, so I couldn't have dreamed it up, could I?"

Jay frowned. "I suppose not."

"In other words, it proves that I definitely saw the Raven — or rather his ghost — when I looked out of my window that night. So *now* do you believe me?"

He said slowly, "Well, yes — I suppose I must."

We carried on walking back to school, me triumphant, Jay rather quiet.

It was okay being proved right about the ghost in broad daylight, but not so good when I lay in bed that night, trying to get to sleep. At least I now had curtains to shut out whatever might be lurking in the garden, but I still couldn't shut out the noises.

Our old house had never made noises — or if it did I must have grown so used to them that I no longer noticed. But End House creaked and groaned for hours after we'd all gone to bed, like a rheumatic old man settling down for the night. I buried my head under the bedclothes, trying not to listen, until eventually I began to drift off to sleep.

Suddenly I awoke with a start.

There was a new sound, quite distinct from anything made by the hot-water pipes.

Footsteps . . .

I sat up in bed, listening. They were outside on the landing, soft, stealthy. Don't be an idiot, Alex, I told myself: it's Mum or Dad creeping to the toilet and trying not to wake anybody. Or maybe Harry Tate . . .

But the footsteps didn't stop at the bathroom. They kept going till they came to my door — then they stopped. I held my breath.

When I heard the sound of a door handle being turned, I groped for the bedside lamp and switched it on. My eyes went straight to my bedroom door, half expecting to see it begin to open, but it didn't. Instead there was a strange noise, like a sudden rush of air, and then the footsteps retreated. After that there was silence.

Summoning all my courage, I flung back the quilt, leapt out of bed and went to open the door. Shivering in the cold night air, I put my head outside and looked up and down the landing.

There was nothing there.

But on the floor at my feet lay a black, shiny feather.

Eight

A Sure Sign

"Ghosts don't have footsteps," Jay said, when I told him next morning at school. "They moan and groan and clank chains, but they don't have footsteps."

"This one does. And that's not all." I opened the polythene bag I'd taken from the kitchen and shook the contents out on to the desk. "It left this outside my bedroom door."

Jay stared down at it. "It's a feather." He picked it up and studied it. "I suppose it could have come from that bird hanging in your hall."

"Yes, it could. But what I'd like to know is, how did it get outside my bedroom door?"

"Perhaps it was blown there. You said you heard a sort of rushing wind."

"Not wind, exactly." But I found it impossible to describe the sound I'd heard — or to explain why I was now convinced it had been made by the wings of a bird.

Jay was obviously stumped. He went on staring at

41

the feather, twisting it round and round in his fingers until, eventually, he said, "I wish I could see this ghost for myself."

"You can," I said. "I've already asked Mum if you can come and stay this weekend. She said yes, for tomorrow night, provided you have your parents' permission."

Jay's eyes gleamed behind his glasses. "Great!" We can be ghost hunters."

Suddenly the idea of footsteps in the night seemed much less scary. It wouldn't be half as bad if Jay was there with me and we could face the Raven's ghost together. I almost looked forward to it.

On Saturday afternoon, when I got back from swimming at the Leisure Centre, there was a plain white hire van parked outside End House, so I guessed Harry Tate must have been to London to fetch the rest of his stuff. I went indoors to find everyone missing. Then I heard voices in the garden. Emily was helping Harry unload the pigeons into the summerhouse. As soon as she saw me she called, "Alex, come and look. They're beautiful; snow white, with lovely soft feathers."

I went closer. Harry had done a lot of work on the summerhouse in the last few days, replacing some of the windows with wire mesh and putting up perches and nesting boxes. The birds looked more like doves to me than pigeons, but I wasn't sure of the difference anyway. "How many are there?" I asked.

"Six pairs," Harry said. "These two are called Mack and Mabel. Want to hold one?"

He gave me a bird and I took it carefully, stroking a finger over its downy white head. It felt warm and living in my hands, with a tiny heartbeat — quite different from the revolting stuffed birds the Raven had collected. The summerhouse was filled with a soft cooing noise, very peaceful and reassuring.

"You like birds?" Harry asked.

"Some birds," I said. "Where's Mum?"

"Gone shopping," said Emily. She turned to Harry. "Can you make them disappear?"

"Not yet," he said. "They need time to settle down in their new home before I set them to work. Especially Mabel." He soothed the bird he was holding. "She's inclined to be nervous."

Em looked disappointed, but only for a moment. "Now Alex is here," she said, "we could start unloading the rest of your stuff."

He took the other pigeon from me and placed them both on a perch. "That's if Alex doesn't mind giving me a hand?"

I said I'd be glad to. This was one of the times when I found myself liking Harry a lot. Besides, I was curious to see what a magician's gear looked like.

We went round to the van and opened the doors. Inside there were some suitcases and boxes and a wicker basket with the word 'CORVO' painted on the side in large black letters. "What does that mean?" Emily asked.

"It's my stage name," Harry said. "The Great Corvo. That's how I'm billed when I'm appearing at a theatre. Alex, can you grab hold of that leather handle?"

Together we heaved the basket out of the van and up the front path. As soon as we'd set it down in the hall, Emily started fiddling with the strap that fastened the lid.

"*Don't touch!*" Harry's voice was so sharp that Emily jumped and turned bright pink. He went on, "A magician has to guard his secrets. He allows no one else to handle his props, except perhaps his assistant. It's one of the rules of magic."

"Sorry," muttered Emily.

"That's all right." He smiled at her, as if to make up for his sharpness. "But you must promise me never to touch my skip again — and by 'skip' I mean the basket. Okay?"

"I promise."

"Good." He leaned forward to pluck something out of her ear and opened his hand to show her a ping-pong ball. "Look what I've found."

She stared at it in fascination. "How did you do that?"

"Easy when you know how." He winked at me over the top of her head. "Do you think you kids could help me get this skip up the stairs and into the attic?"

"The door's locked," I said.

"Your mother gave me the key."

The skip wasn't all that heavy: at a guess, it contained clothes — probably the costume he used for his stage act. As soon as we arrived in the attic, Harry switched on the light and looked round. "Is this old Cheyney's furniture?" he asked. "Some of it looks rather good."

"That's why Dad didn't want to sell it," I said.

Then Emily said, "He haunts this house."

We both turned to stare at her.

"The Raven," she said, "I think he's still here."

A door slammed down below; Mum's voice called out, "Where is everybody?"

Em went to the top of the attic staircase. "Coming, Mum."

When she'd gone, Harry and I looked at each other. "Your sister has a vivid imagination," he remarked, with a grin.

44

I didn't correct him, although I knew he was wrong. Emily had practically no imagination at all. That's what made it so strange that she should also think the house was haunted. "Let's get the rest of your stuff indoors."

Later, I found Emily alone in the sitting room, her eyes fixed on the television screen. "Em," I said, "I want to talk to you."

"Not now, Alex. I'm watching *EastEnders*."

"This is important." I placed myself between her and the TV set. "Why did you say this house was haunted?"

"Because it is." She peered round me at the screen.

"You must have some reason. Have you seen something?" When she didn't answer, I switched off the sound on the remote control. "You said the Raven was still here. How do you know?"

She shrugged. "I just feel it. Sometimes it gets very cold, especially at night. That's a sure sign there are ghosts around."

"This is a cold house. Old houses are always draughtier than modern ones."

It struck me that I was bringing out the same sort of arguments Jay had used on me. Perhaps this was because I didn't want to believe that Em shared my fears about End House.

"It doesn't worry me," she said. "I like ghosts. So push off, Alex, I want to watch my programme." Seizing the remote control, she switched the sound back on again.

Tonight, I thought, Jay will be here — and then maybe we'll bust this thing once and for all.

Nine

Ghosthunters

"I can't see a thing," Jay said, peering into the garden. He was kneeling on the folding bed, which we'd put up over by the window, and I'd switched off the lamp so that we could see better in the dark. "Where am I supposed to be looking?"

"By the laurel bush," I told him.

"I can't even *see* the laurel bush. It's pitch black out there."

He was right. There was no moon and the garden was almost invisible. I said, "We may as well draw the curtains and wait for the footsteps."

"Okay."

We settled down, sitting cross-legged on the floor.

"Let's check our equipment," said Jay. "Torch?"

"Torch."

"Sheet for throwing over ghost's head when we catch it?"

"Sheet," I repeated, doubtfully, "although I don't think it'll be much good. Ghosts are spirits. Even if

46

we get near enough to throw the sheet over it'll probably disappear."

"Well, that's what you want, isn't it? You want it to disappear."

"Yes, but for good, not just for the time being. To do that you have to have them exercised."

"You mean *exorcised*," Jay corrected.

"Whatever; anyway, it has to be done by experts."

"Okay, but first you have to prove . . ."

"Sssh!"

"What?"

"Listen . . ."

We held our breaths. The footsteps came along the landing and stopped outside my door as before. I couldn't see Jay's face because we were still in the dark but I knew he was as tense as I was. Then came a small metallic click.

"What's that?" Jay hissed.

"It sounded like a door catch. Maybe someone's gone up to the attic." I tried to remember if Harry had locked it after we'd been up there this afternoon, but couldn't.

"In that case it can't be a ghost," Jay said. "Ghosts don't need to open doors."

"No," I agreed. But I still didn't move.

Jay said, "It's probably your father. Or maybe your lodger — you said he'd put some stuff in the attic today. Maybe he just thought of something he needed."

"In the middle of the night?"

"Well, then it must be a burglar."

This was not a comforting thought: the Raven had been a burglar. Perhaps he still liked to keep his hand in, even though he was now a ghost?

Jay said, "Don't you think we ought to check."

He switched on the torch and I opened the door. The torch beam showed us that the landing was empty and the door to the attic stairs closed. "I must have been wrong," I said.

"Or they may have shut it behind them," Jay said. "Let's take a look."

The door was unlocked. I went up the stairs first, switching on the light as soon as I set foot in the attic. "Wow!" said Jay, arriving just behind me. "It looks like a junk shop. Did all this stuff belong to the Raven?"

"Most of it." I turned to go. "Well, there's obviously nobody here, so . . ."

"Hang on a minute." He stared round at the upturned dining-room chairs, the chest of drawers, the cases of stuffed birds stacked on the table. "We haven't checked properly yet."

"Be careful," I warned. "Dad says some of the floorboards are dodgy. If you fall through . . ."

"I won't. What's in this basket?"

"It belongs to Harry Tate. Leave it alone, Jay, he doesn't like people touching his props."

"Okay. Well, I suppose . . ." He broke off, listening. ". . . sounds like someone's coming up the stairs."

We both stood still, not daring to move.

Emily's face appeared in the hatchway. "Alex? Is that you?"

I groaned. "Oh, Em! Go back to bed."

"Why should I?" Hitching up her red quilted dressing gown she scrambled into the loft. "If you two are up to something, I want to be in on it. What are you doing here?"

"None of your business. Anyway, we've finished."

"I know!" she said, triumphantly. "You're looking

for the ghost, aren't you? You heard the noises too."

Jay and I exchanged a look. I said, "What noises, Em?"

"Oh, the creaks and footsteps and things."

"Footsteps?"

She nodded, her eyes shining. "Isn't it great? I've always wanted to live in a house that's haunted. Do you think we'll ever get to see him? The Raven, I mean."

Jay said, "Alex has already seen him."

Em's mouth dropped open. "No! What does he look like."

I glared at Jay, but he took no notice. "According to Alex, he has a face like a bird. You know, with little beady eyes and a hooked beak instead of a nose."

"Alex! Why didn't you tell me?"

"Look, let's leave it, shall we?" I said. "I'm not absolutely certain I saw him. As Jay said, it may have been a trick of the light."

"But what about the footsteps?"

"Well, there's probably some other explanation for those. I think we should go back to bed before anyone hears us."

"Wait a minute," said Emily. "While we're up here, couldn't we — you know?" she jerked her head in the direction of the skip.

"No," I said. All I wanted was to get out of the loft and safely back to bed before we were caught.

"Oh, go on, Alex; just a quick look. I'm dying to see what's inside." She started to unfasten the leather strap. "Harry will never know."

I'm not sure exactly what happened next, but the electric light started flickering on and off and then there was the most almighty crash. We all stood frozen to the spot.

Eventually the light stopped flickering and came back on again properly. I stared at the floor. The showcase containing the stuffed owl had fallen off the table, breaking the glass and scattering feathers everywhere.

Then Dad's voice came from below us, on the landing. "What the heck's going on up there?"

Ten

Postmortem

"I'm not surprised you knocked it off the table," Mum said, next morning at breakfast. "Barging around the attic in the middle of the night like that. Honestly, Alex!"

"It wasn't Alex who knocked it off," Emily protested, her mouth full of toast. "He wasn't anywhere near it. So it must have . . ."

I kicked her, hard, under the table. She shut up at once. I'll say this for Emily, for all her 'satiable curtiosity' she's not a complete idiot.

"Poor Mr Tate," Mum went on. "He must think he's come to live in a madhouse, with all that bumping and crashing going on in the night."

"Didn't hear a thing," Harry said cheerfully, tucking into his bacon and eggs. "But then I'm a very heavy sleeper. Nothing wakes me once I've dropped off."

Jay said, "I'm like that. I can sleep through anything except a thunderstorm."

"Why a thunderstorm?" Emily asked.

Jay didn't immediately answer. He took a sip of tea and mumbled, "I don't like lightning."

I guessed this probably had something to do with his fear of fire and was therefore rather a touchy subject. To draw attention away from him I asked Mum, "Was Dad very angry?"

"Furious," she said. "You know how important it is for him to get a good night's sleep, especially as he's been working on a very difficult case all week."

"What case is that?" asked Emily.

Mum gave her a quelling look; we weren't supposed to discuss Dad's work, especially in front of outsiders like Jay and Harry. But Em wouldn't let the matter rest. "Oh, I know," she went on, "I bet it's that man who's been going round telling old people he's come to read their gas meters, and then he robs them of their savings. I saw it on the local news. Horrible man, I hope Dad catches him soon."

Mum changed the subject. "What I don't understand is why you all went up to the attic in the first place. Were you looking for something?"

"Not really," I said. "We just sort of — er . . ."

"Wanted an adventure," Jay cut in.

Mum sighed. "Oh well, I suppose there was no real harm done — apart from that wretched owl, and I can't pretend I'm sorry that's gone. So we'll say no more about it." She looked at Jay and me. "Except that I'd like to know what you're planning to do this morning?"

"Nothing much," I said. "Harry, could I show Jay the pigeons?"

"Okay, Alex. You can feed them, if you like, the way I showed you yesterday. You know where the bag of corn mixture is?"

"Yeah. Thanks."

In the summerhouse, Jay said, "Your lodger seems a decent sort of a bloke, although . . ." He hesitated.

"Although what?"

"It's odd that he's the only one who never showed up last night. Your father heard us, and your mother, but there was no sign of Mr Tate."

"That's because he's a heavy sleeper. You heard what he said, he slept through everything."

"With all that racket going on? Glass breaking, your father yelling at us — nobody could have slept through that."

"What are you suggesting, Jay? That he was up there in the attic all the time, hiding from us?"

"It's possible."

"But why should he bother to hide? He had as much right to be there as we had. Anyway, it still doesn't explain the lights flickering and the owl falling off the table."

"He's a magician, isn't he?"

I refilled the pigeons' drinking bowl and shook some grit into the hopper, the way Harry had shown me. Glancing through the window, I saw Emily coming up the path towards us and warned Jay, "Watch out, there's a female alien approaching."

She stuck her head round the door. "Are you having a postmortem?"

"A what?" asked Jay.

"A postmortem, talking over what happened last night. It's police jargon. I'm good at police jargon. Well, I have to be, as I'm going to be a policewoman." She added, "That's if I don't become a magician's assistant instead."

Jay grinned. "There's not much difference!"

She ignored him. "Actually, I came to tell you some fantastic news. You know it's my birthday in two weeks' time? Well, Mum's always said before I couldn't have a large party because we didn't have the space, but now we do have the space so she's said okay as long as it's not too many and I've asked Harry if he'll do a magic show and he's said yes! What do you think of *that*, Alex? Of course you won't be able to come to the tea but you can come to the show afterwards, if you like, and bring Jay as well, but that's all. We don't want too many boys. Oh, and get this — Harry says I can be his assistant and hand him the pigeons and things!" Breathless, she waited for our reaction.

"Sounds great," I said.

"Yes, isn't it? I can't wait to tell Debbie Grover, she'll be green with envy. In fact I think I'll go and tell her now." She disappeared, but two seconds later she stuck her head round the door again. "About your postmortem — it couldn't have been the ghost who knocked the owl off the table."

"Why not?" I asked.

"Because it didn't go cold. I told you before, it always goes cold when there's a ghost around. So I reckon Jay must have jogged it. He was the only one standing close enough to the table." She went again.

Jay said, "It wasn't me who jogged it."

"Maybe not, but I still can't believe it was Harry."

Jay grinned. "You're so determined to prove your ghost theory you'll talk yourself into anything. But if I were you I'd keep my eye on that lodger of yours. He's the real mystery around here, if you ask me."

Eleven

Mystery Man

During the next few days I thought a lot about what Jay had said. It made me watch Harry more closely. The trouble was, of course, that I was at school during the day, so I had no idea how he occupied his time.

After tea on Wednesday I found Mum alone in the dining room, writing letters. "Mum," I said, "what do you think Harry does all day here by himself?"

Only half listening, she replied, "I've no idea, Alex. He's usually working in the garden when I get back from the Medical Centre, digging up those overgrown flower beds near the summerhouse. I must say it was a real stroke of luck, finding a lodger who's also a keen gardener. Heaven knows I don't have the time to do it."

It seemed somehow surprising, when I stopped to think about it, that Harry should be so keen on gardening. He didn't strike me as being the outdoor type, maybe because of his pale complexion. But of course that was due to his illness, so perhaps he was now trying to get himself fit again.

I said, "We still don't know much about him, do we? He never talks about his past or . . ."

I was interrupted by a shriek from Emily. "Mum, Alex, come quickly! Dad's on the telly."

Mum threw down her pen and we both dashed into the living room. Harry was playing patience on the card table, Emily kneeling on the floor close to the TV set. "He's on the local news, talking about the con man," she said. "He's warning people not to let him into their homes."

Dad's screen image seemed unfamiliar, sterner and stiffer than he was in real life. ". . . can't rule out the possibility there may be more than one operator," he was saying. "So far we have three conflicting descriptions, of a man with black hair and glasses, a short man with a bald head, and a fair man with a moustache. However, in each case the method of gaining entry has been very similar, which leads us to suspect there must be a link between the three cases."

"Do you have any advice to give the public?" asked the interviewer. "Especially the elderly, since they seem to be most at risk."

"Yes, I have." Dad spoke directly to the camera. "If anyone calls at your door, no matter how convincing they may be, ask to see identification. If you're in any doubt at all, don't let them into your house, but go and telephone the gas company, or the water board, or whoever they claim to represent."

"Thank you, Inspector. And now, back to the studio."

Emily turned off the sound. "Wasn't he brilliant?" she said. "I do hope Debbie Grover was watching."

Mum said, "Let's hope the broadcast did some

good. If it puts people on their guard, that's the important thing."

"I quite agree," said Harry. "How anyone can stoop so low as to rob old people, I can't imagine." He picked up the cards and shuffled them. "Care for a game of gin rummy, Alex?"

"Okay." I joined him at the table. Emily came to watch us.

He beat me hollow. I knew he was cheating — and he knew that I knew, that's why he was grinning all over his face. But I couldn't catch him at it.

"He's doing magic," Emily said, when we finished the third hand. "It's a good thing you're not playing for money, Alex."

"Quite right." Harry picked up the cards and put them away in a box. "So let that be a lesson to you, Alex — never play cards with a magician. May I have that ace of hearts back, please?"

"I don't have it," I said.

"Yes, you do." He took a card out of my shirt pocket and flipped it over to show it was the ace of hearts. "Now the queen — and the jack . . ."

He went on producing cards seemingly out of nowhere. Emily watched him like a lynx. "Where are you hiding them?" she demanded. "Are they up your sleeve?"

"Can't you tell?" Pulling up his sleeve, he put out his hand palm facing us, turned it to show the back, then over again to reveal the ace of spades. "This is called prestidigitation. Anyone can do it with a little practice."

I said, "There's a blister on your hand. Did you get it from digging in the garden?"

"What? Oh — yes, I suppose I must have done." He gave me a sharp look. "How did you know I'd

57

been digging in the garden?"

"Mum told me. She said it was a piece of luck, having a lodger who was keen on gardening."

His lips twitched. "Did she now?" He turned to Emily. "Are you still keen to be my assistant for your birthday magic show?"

"You bet!"

He grinned at her. "In that case, we'd better get in some practice. After all, your party's only ten days away. Tomorrow we'll start rehearsals."

Emily went pink with pleasure.

I spent the rest of that evening watching Harry, without being too obvious about it. On the face of it he seemed, as Jay had said, a decent sort of bloke; yet there was something about him that didn't quite add up. Why had he come to Bursley, for a start?

And why was he content to hang around End House all day, digging up the garden and looking after his pigeons? You'd think he'd need to get some kind of job so that he could pay the rent. Okay, so he was still recovering from his illness, whatever it was, but it seemed strange that he received no letters and nobody ever called him on the telephone.

Maybe Jay was right to call him a mystery.

That night I awoke with a start, conscious that some kind of noise had disturbed my sleep. I lay still, listening hard.

It came again, a furtive little scratching at my door.

I put out my hand to switch on the lamp but nothing happened. The bulb must have blown. "Em?" I said. "Is that you?"

No reply.

Could it be mice? But it wasn't a mouse-like sound.

58

Mice rustle and scrabble, this sounded more like the pecking of a beak . . .

I leapt out of bed and flung open the door.

At first I couldn't see anything. Then, in a shaft of moonlight streaming through the landing window, I saw a dark shape standing motionless on the floor, near the top of the stairs. It was a bird, with wings outstretched and head cocked on one side, staring at me.

The Raven!

Twelve

The Real Ghost

I shot back into my room and closed the door, breathing as hard as if I'd just run a three-minute mile. My heartbeats were so loud I could hear them.

Then I started to think.

There had been something unnatural about that bird. Despite having its wings outstretched, it had been motionless. What's more, I seemed to recognize it . . .

It was the stuffed raven that hung on the wall over the front door!

But how had it got on to the landing?

And was it still there?

To know the answer, I'd have to open the door. What was I afraid of, anyway — being attacked by a stuffed bird? Surely this was my chance to prove I wasn't a coward, that I could be as brave as my father if I had to face danger.

Yes, but physical danger was one thing — the supernatural quite another.

Then I remembered what Emily had said. *It always goes cold when there are ghosts around*. And it wasn't particularly cold, no more than you'd expect in the middle of the night in early October. So maybe there was nothing supernatural about it . . .

Well, I couldn't go on arguing with myself all night. If I was going to do something I had to do it, right away. Luckily I still had the torch Jay and I had used. I took it out of my bedside locker and gripped it firmly, steeling myself to open the door.

The landing was empty.

I crept along to the top of the stairs. The moonlight was bright enough for me to find my way without having to switch on the torch. Cautiously I went down the first few steps until I could see into the hall. The light slanting through the narrow side window showed me someone on the stepladder, fixing the stuffed raven back on the wall.

I knew at once that it was Harry Tate. It couldn't have been Dad, he wasn't tall enough. What's more, the light was shining on the little bald patch in the middle of his head. I sat down on the stair, peering through the bannisters to watch him. His magician's hands were making easy work of reconnecting the wires that operated the burglar alarm. And of course that explained why my bedside lamp wouldn't work — he must have switched off the electricity.

But why should Harry want to play such a trick? Just for fun, the way he'd cheated me at cards?

I was about to challenge him, when suddenly there came that strange rush of air I'd felt before. Harry, still on the ladder, looked round sharply. There was a beating sound over my head, like wings, and a dark shadow swooped down the stairs. It flew across the beam of moonlight, so low that Harry had to duck, and gave a harsh cry before disappearing through the door into the living room. Recovering his balance, Harry shook his fist and said something aloud. It sounded like, "You don't scare me, you old buzzard!"

It was then that I realized my fingers, clutching the upright struts of the bannister, were frozen stiff. In fact I was shivering all over. It felt as if the whole house had suddenly been plunged into the Ice Age.

It always goes cold when there are ghosts around.

Without waiting for anything else I fled back into my room, shut the door and leapt into bed. About ten minutes later, when I'd stopped shivering, I tried the bedside lamp again. It worked.

"Let me get this straight," Jay said, when I told him in the playground next morning, on our way into school. "You now think there are two ghosts — a fake one and a real one?"

"Something like that."

"And the fake one is really your lodger playing tricks? So it's his footsteps we heard — and he who knocked the stuffed owl off the table in the loft?"

I nodded.

"Well, of course I thought that all along. And he must have overheard us talking about the Raven's ghost, which gave him the idea of putting the stuffed bird outside your room. But what I don't understand is *why*?"

I said with a shrug, "His idea of a joke, I s'pose."

At this point the bell rang for morning school so we had to go into the classroom. While Miss Passmore was taking the register we carried on our conversation in whispers, behind our maths books.

"What was it you said he said," Jay hissed, "after the ghost had disappeared?"

" 'You don't scare me, you old buzzard.' And that's not all. Next morning when I came downstairs I went into the living room, and in front of the fireplace I found this." Under cover of the desk I showed him the polythene bag. It now contained two feathers.

"Alexander Mackay!" Miss Passmore's voice made me jump. "Have you gone deaf? I've called your name out twice."

"Oh — sorry, Miss Passmore." Hastily, I shoved the polythene bag into my desk.

She marked the register. "Jay Nimrod?"

"Here, Miss Passmore."

We didn't get a chance to talk during the next two lessons but, at breaktime, Jay took me aside in the playground and asked, "Are you going to tell your parents?"

"Don't be stupid. They wouldn't believe me."

"I didn't mean about the ghost; about your lodger."

"What's there to tell? That he likes playing tricks on people? He's a magician, isn't he? He spends his whole life playing tricks."

Jay said, "Aren't you at least going to let him know that you caught him out last night?"

"I might do," I said. "On the other hand I might keep quiet about it and try to get my own back on him sometime. In fact, I've got an idea already."

"What's that?"

"I'll tell you if it works out," I replied, mysteriously.

Thirteen

Looking for a Bird's Nest?

That afternoon, when I got home from school, I went straight into the living room and put the feather back where I'd found it, in front of the hearth. I prayed hard Emily wouldn't see it first, before I'd had a chance to play out the little scene I'd planned for Harry Tate, but luckily she went out after tea to Brownies. Mum took her in the car.

When I went back to the living room, Harry was already there, reading the *Gazette*. He didn't seem to have noticed the feather because it was still lying where I'd placed it.

"Hello," I said. "What's that doing there?"

"Mmmm?" He looked up from the newspaper.

"This feather." I picked it up and held it out for him to see.

He stared at it for quite a while before saying, "Looks like there's been a bird in here." He got out of his chair and came over to where I was standing by the fireplace. "Could have flown up the chimney, I suppose."

I noticed he said 'flown *up* the chimney', which seemed to me a dead giveaway; most people would have taken it for granted that the bird had come *down* the chimney, unless they'd seen what both Harry and I had seen last night.

I decided to push him a little further. "Harry," I said, "do you believe in ghosts?"

His lips twitched. "Of course. Don't you?"

I said, "This house is haunted, you know, by the man who used to live here, the one they called the Raven." I watched his face carefully as I spoke. "The other night someone tried to play a trick on me by putting the stuffed raven from the hall outside my bedroom door, but of course I knew it wasn't the real ghost because it didn't move. And the real ghost usually leaves a feather behind — like this one." I held out the feather in my hand.

Harry gave me a long, hard look. Then he said, "I can see you're not easily scared, Alex, not even by ghosts. And that's good. Because it's what they want, you know, to scare you off — and if someone tries to do that it's usually because they have something to hide."

I stared at him. "What sort of thing?"

"Ah, now that's what we have to ask ourselves, isn't it?" He peered up the chimney. "When did you last have this swept?"

"We haven't yet, not since we moved in. Mum says it's too soon to start lighting fires."

"The evenings are starting to get colder, though. If she wants the chimney swept I don't mind doing it for her."

When he suggested this to Mum, after lunch on Sunday, she laughed and said, "Really, Mr Tate, is

65

there no end to your talents?"

"It doesn't take much talent to sweep a chimney," he replied. "I daresay there's a tool-hire firm around here who'd supply me with a vacuum machine. If you can find some old sheets to cover the furniture we're in business."

Mum said, "Sounds like an offer we can't refuse. Doesn't it, Colin?"

Dad grunted, half-hidden behind the Sunday paper. We'd all just eaten a huge meal of roast lamb, followed by apple pie and cream, and were now sprawled out in the living room, hardly able to move.

I said to Harry, "I'll help you clean the chimney."

"You'll be at school, young Alex."

"No, I won't. It's half term; I'll be home all week."

This didn't please him — I could tell by the way his lips twitched and then tightened. But he smiled at me pleasantly enough. "Okay," he said. "You can be the sweep's assistant."

"Like I'm the magician's assistant," said Emily. "Mum, can we talk about my costume, please? The party's next Saturday and I don't have anything to wear for the magic show."

Mum looked harassed. "What sort of costume?"

"Someting silvery, with spangles on it. Oh, and fishnet tights. All magicians' assistants wear fishnet tights; don't they, Harry?"

"Er — yes, I believe they do." He smiled, apologetically, at Mum.

"Oh, very well," she said, with a sigh. "I'll see what I can find."

Someone snored. We all looked at Dad. The newspaper had fallen over his face and his chest was rising and falling with deep, regular breaths. Mum smiled. "He's worn out," she said. "Let him rest."

66

Emily went on, "Anyway, I've learned a lot about magic. Mum, I'll bet you've never heard of misdirection?"

"Keep your voice down, Em," Mum said, "or you'll wake your father."

"What's misdirection?" I asked.

It was Harry who answered. "Misdirection, Alex, is the device whereby a magician fools the audience into watching the wrong piece of action, so they don't notice what's going on elsewhere."

Emily beamed at him. "Isn't that great? I'm getting good with the pigeons too. Mack flies to my finger now as soon as he's released. Mabel doesn't yet, she's still too nervous, but I think she will by the end of the week. Please, Harry — can we go out to the summerhouse now and rehearse some more?"

"For heaven's sake," Mum said, "give poor Mr Tate time to recover after his dinner or he'll have indigestion."

"It's okay," he said. "Come on, young Emily."

When they'd gone I asked Mum, "Do you like him?"

She looked surprised. "Mr Tate? Yes, of course. I must say he seems to have endless patience with Emily — and if he's prepared to sweep the chimney for us I shall be only too pleased." She lowered her voice. "Just between ourselves, Alex, this house is beginning to get me down."

"Do you wish we hadn't come to live here?"

She glanced at Dad to make sure he was still asleep. "In some ways, yes. I was against the idea from the start, if you remember, but your father was so keen that I've tried to make the best of it, for his sake. To be honest, though, it still doesn't feel like home. In fact it gives me the shivers."

I was about to ask if she thought it was haunted when Dad stirred and pushed the newspaper away from his face. "What gives you the shivers?" he inquired.

Without batting an eyelid Mum said, "The thought of those wretched con men going round Bursley, deceiving people. Are you any nearer catching them yet?"

"As a matter of fact, we may have a lead at last, although it isn't certain." Dad yawned. "Where's Emily gone?"

"She's dragged the long suffering Mr Tate out to the summerhouse again, to rehearse their magic act. Oh, and Colin, he's offered to sweep this chimney for us. I said yes, please."

"Is that wise?" Dad asked. "Sweeping chimneys can be a messy job. Surely it's best left to the professionals?"

"He's going to hire the proper equipment. Anyway, I get the impression he knows what he's doing — and it'll save us money, which is the main consideration."

Dad shrugged. "Okay, Pam, have it your way."

The following Tuesday Harry collected the vacuum cleaner from a local tool-hire company, using the white van he still hadn't returned after his London trip. We covered the furniture and carpet in the living room with old sheets, and spread newspaper over the floor round the hearth. Then he set to work.

He made a slow, very thorough job of it, stopping every now and again to check the soot already sucked down the tube into the metal drum. Slightly puzzled by this, I asked him what he was looking for.

"Can't be too careful, old son," he said. "You never know what you might find up a chimney."

"Like a bird's nest?" I suggested, tongue in cheek.

"That's right." His lips twitched. "A bird's nest is exactly what we're looking for, preferably with a few eggs inside, waiting to be hatched." He switched on the vacuum again for a short burst, then switched it off and checked the drum, "Nothing here," he said. "No bird's nest, no feathers, no ghosts; reckon we might as well call it a day."

He didn't speak to me while we were clearing up the living room, and I could tell from his face that he was in a bad mood again. Whatever he'd hoped to find up the chimney, he'd been disappointed.

But somehow I had the feeling it wasn't a bird's nest.

Fourteen

The Magic Show

"I don't like magic shows," Jay said, as we walked home from the Leisure Centre, our damp swimming gear in bags slung over our shoulders. "They always follow the same routine — a few card tricks, masses of scarves conjured out of a hat and then the big finale."

"In that case, why are you coming?" I asked.

"Because I'm curious to see if your lodger's any good at it." He grinned. "Besides, there might be some tea left over, if we're lucky."

"After fifteen girls have got there first? You must be joking!"

I was right about the tea. The dining room looked as if it had been hit by a fifty megaton bomb and Mum was still clearing away the debris when we arrived. "You're just in time," she said, "Mr Tate's about to start any minute so you'd better hurry on into the living room and grab a seat." As we left the room she added, "By the way, I managed to save you some birthday cake. You'll find it on the kitchen table."

"Thanks, Mum." We collected the cake on our way to the living room, so we could eat it during the show.

The living room was packed with girls, all shapes and sizes, occupying every available chair. As soon as they saw us they started to giggle and nudge each other. "It's okay," Emily shouted. "I said Alex and Jay could come, as long as they promised to behave themselves."

At the far end of the living room, in front of the bay window, a space had been cleared to make a stage. Behind it the red velvet curtains had been drawn, although it was still daylight outside, and on the right of the stage stood our card table with a blue cloth over it. On the left-hand side was a black screen covered with silver stars.

"Where's Mr Tate?" Jay whispered, as we took a couple of chairs at the back of the room.

"Waiting to make a dramatic entrance, I expect."

At this point I was shushed fiercely by some girls in the next row, and realized that Emily had stood up to make the introduction. She was wearing a frilled ballet skirt over a pink lycra catsuit — her birthday present from Mum and Dad — and had a tinsel crown on her head. It made her look more like something out of a pantomime than a magician's assistant but, judging from the oohs and aahs of the girls around us, they thought she looked terrific.

"Ladies and gentlemen," she announced, grinning all over her face. "Now we've got a special treat. A real magician, who's going to do the most amazing stuff right before your eyes. So here he is, the Master of Mystery and Illusion . . ." She waved her hand towards the screen and almost yelled the last three words: ". . . The Great Corvo!"

I hardly recognized the man who stepped on to the stage. Not only was he wearing a black suit with long coat tails, a starched white shirt, white bow tie and gloves, but he also had black hair, a moustache and a neat little black beard. For a moment I thought there must have been some mistake; then he smiled and I saw that it was indeed Harry Tate.

"Some disguise!" Jay mumbled beside me, his mouth full of cake.

The first part of the act was, as Jay had predicted, pretty routine stuff, such as pulling bunches of flowers out of a top hat, producing eggs from people's ears and making glasses of milk disappear.

"I know how that's done," Jay said. "It was in a magician's handbook I had for Christmas once."

The girl in front of us turned her head to give Jay a withering look. "Emily said you were only allowed in here as long as you behaved," she said. "So shut up!" Jay waited until she'd turned round again, then pulled a face and waggled his ears at her.

Harry was saying, ". . . you'll all have heard of Houdini, I'm sure. He was what we call an 'escapologist' — that's someone who specializes in escaping from impossible situations. Now I'm something of an escapologist myself, as I'm going to prove to you. First, I need an upright chair, like that one . . ." He pointed to a dining-room chair. Emily pushed the girl who was sitting on it off and carried it forward to the stage.

Harry sat down and handed her a length of rope, asking her to tie one end securely round his wrist. He bent forward so that she could pass the rope under the chair and tie it to his other wrist, then told Emily to place the screen in front of him and count to ten.

"That's cheating," Jay muttered. "When she takes

the screen away again he'll be free and standing up, you'll see."

But when Emily removed the screen, Harry was still sitting in the chair with his wrists tied and the rope in place. The only difference was that he was no longer wearing his coat. It was hanging over the back of the chair.

Everyone clapped like mad.

Harry asked Emily to untie him and took a bow. Then he put on his coat again and made a great show of complaining that it didn't fit so well as it had done before. "There's something here," he said, and reached inside to produce a pigeon. The bird fluttered its wings and flew to Emily's hand. She placed it on a perch at the side of the stage. Then Harry produced more pigeons from all over the place until, finally, he threw a silk scarf up in the air and that turned into a pigeon as well. When Emily had put it with the others on the perch I counted them. All six pairs were there. So the hours of practice Emily had put in with the nervous Mabel must have paid off.

Harry stepped forward. "Now, usually that's the end of the show, but as this is Emily's birthday I have something rather special up my sleeve. Something, in fact, that she knows nothing about, so it'll be just as much a surprise to her as to the rest of you."

A murmur of anticipation went round the audience.

He lowered his voice. "I wonder how many of you know that this house is haunted?"

Somebody giggled, nervously.

"It's true," Emily spoke up. "There *is* a ghost. My brother, Alex, has seen it."

Fifteen heads screwed round to stare at me. I felt myself turning red.

"Shall we find out how brave you all are," Harry

asked. "Would you like to see the ghost?"

Some of the girls murmured excitedly, but most of them stayed silent.

"What's he playing at?" Jay muttered, in my ear. "He's scaring them half to death."

"It's just part of the act," I said, although I was beginning to feel a little uneasy myself.

"Let's leave the decision to Emily," Harry said. "She's the birthday girl. Well, Emily — do *you* want to see the ghost?"

Just for a moment, she hesitated. Then she said, "Yes — yes, please." When the audience started to babble she raised her voice and shouted, "It's okay, it'll only be an illusion. Go on, Harry."

He smiled at her. "Very well. But you must all keep very quiet . . ."

They kept quiet all right. You could have heard a pin drop.

Then the light went out.

A couple of girls squealed, but they were quickly shushed.

"How'd he do that?" Jay whispered. "Nobody was standing anywhere near the switch."

I didn't answer. My eyes were fixed on the stage where, slowly, something was taking shape, glowing luminously in the dark. A long drawn-out "Aaah!" went round the room, and I almost laughed aloud.

It was just an ordinary old skeleton.

Once it might have scared me, but now it didn't have any power. It wasn't the Raven, that's all I was worried about. I should have known Harry wouldn't pull a trick like that.

Then I felt a sudden icy draught and a girl screamed, "There's something flying round the room."

"It's a bat — I heard its wings!"
"I felt it too. It touched my hair!"
At that point pandemonium broke out.

Fifteen

Misdirection

I leapt for the light switch, but it went on just before I got there. Mum was standing in the open doorway. "What on earth's going on?" she demanded.

"Calm down, everyone!" Emily shouted. "There's nothing to be afraid of. Look . . ."

On stage, Harry was holding a piece of black material on which was painted a skeleton. He looked a bit uncomfortable, I thought. Obviously this mass hysteria wasn't quite the reaction he'd expected, which made me think perhaps he wasn't all that used to giving magic shows in front of kids.

"But the bat . . ."

"It touched my hair!"

"I felt its wings . . ."

Emily said, scornfully, "That wasn't a bat, it was one of the pigeons. Look — Mabel's missing. I expect she was frightened by the noise."

"I'm not surprised," Mum said. "Is the show over now?"

"Yes, all over." Harry seemed to have recovered. He started putting the rest of the pigeons into a cage. "Could somebody please catch Mabel for me?"

"She's not here," Emily said. "She must have flown out of the room when Mum opened the door."

"I'll go and look for her," I said, glad of the excuse to escape from the roomful of squeaking, chattering girls. Mum was still trying to calm them down when I went into the hall.

I saw Mabel at once. She was sitting on the newel post at the end of the bannister, preening her ruffled feathers, but as soon as I started toward her she flew off up the stairs. I followed her. For a moment she seemed almost within my grasp when she touched down briefly on the landing but, as soon as she saw me, she took off again. As luck would have it the door to the attic was open — Harry must have left it like that after he'd fetched his gear — so Mabel flew right up the second flight of stairs.

Well, at least I now had her cornered.

I followed her into the attic. It was the first time I'd been up here since the night Jay and I had come in search of the ghost. Dad had been careful to keep the door locked since then.

Mabel was perched on the skip, watching me with a wary eye as I advanced. "It's all right, Mabel," I murmured, "I'm not going to hurt you."

She let me get close. Then, just as I reached out my hand to her she took flight again, whirring round the room. Taken by surprise, I almost overbalanced, falling against the skip.

That was when I noticed the leather strap was undone.

Even then I didn't open the skip, not straight away. Harry had been so insistent that nobody should touch it; and that night, when Emily had been about to unfasten the lid, the owl had crashed to the floor. According to Jay, it was Harry who'd made that happen. Then I remembered what Harry had said about misdirection — the device whereby a magician fools the audience into watching the wrong piece of action.

Why didn't he want us to look inside the skip?

I lifted the lid. As I'd first thought, it was full of clothes. But they weren't all stage costumes. Some of them were quite ordinary clothes: jeans, leather jackets, workmen's overalls.

There was also a metal box with a padlock attached to it. The padlock was open. I took the box out of the basket and looked inside. It contained stage make-up; but not only make-up, there was also a compartment filled with bits of false hair, together with a tube of glue, as well as a plastic bag full of wigs.

"Alex?"

It was Harry's voice, coming from the bottom of the attic stairs, and it sounded sharp. I called back quickly, "Yes, I'm here — and so's Mabel. I'm trying to catch her, but she won't let me get close enough."

"Okay, I'm coming up."

Hastily, I shoved the box back into the skip and closed the lid. By the time Harry reached the top of the stairs I was on the other side of the attic, pretending to be in pursuit of Mabel.

Harry whistled softly. She flew to him at once.

"I followed her up the stairs," I said, talking fast to cover my nervousness. Had he guessed what I'd been doing? He had that bad tempered look again, for all he was being gentle with Mabel. "It was lucky I saw her fly into the attic, otherwise we mightn't have known she was here."

"Yes, it was," he said shortly, turning to go.

He went down the stairs first, carrying Mabel on his finger, and I followed him. When we reached the landing he turned away without saying a word. But there was one question I had to ask.

"Harry . . ."

He stopped. "Yes?"

"Why did you do that trick about the ghost? Didn't you guess the girls would be scared?"

He gave me a long, considering look. Then he smiled. "Call it an error of judgement, Alex. It was only meant to be a bit of fun. I thought Emily would like it, knowing this house is supposed to be haunted."

"Oh," I said. "I thought maybe it was another piece of — what did you call it — misdirection?"

He stopped smiling. "Did you indeed? I'll say this for you, young Alex, you're a lot sharper than you look. Come on, let's get Mabel back inside her cage."

We went downstairs, to find that Mum had managed to restore order just as the girls' mothers started to arrive to take them home. Most of the girls were raving on about what a fantastic time they'd had, so I supposed the ghost trick must have been a success after all. They clustered round Mabel, saying wasn't she sweet and how stupid of Debbie or Sarah or Susan to be scared of a little old pigeon. When Emily had seen them off, and Harry had taken the pigeons out to the summerhouse, I went into the living room to find Jay sitting by himself, staring into space.

"Whew!" I said, collapsing into a chair beside him. "What a racket. They say boys are noisy, but I reckon we're quiet compared to a gang of eight-year-old girls."

Jay said, "How did he do it?"

"The ghost trick? It was luminous paint; I guessed that as soon as I saw it. It wasn't very convincing, anyway."

"I didn't mean the skeleton, Alex. I meant the raven."

"That wasn't the raven, it was Mabel. I caught her upstairs in the attic."

Jay shook his head. "Mabel's feathers are white. I found this one . . ." He held out his hand. ". . . lying on the floor, after everyone had gone."

The feather he showed me was black.

It was only then I remembered the icy draught of air that had swept through the room just after we were plunged into darkness.

Sixteen

Deadly Enemies

I was glad it was Jay who'd found the black feather, because I could see that at last he was beginning to take me seriously. He'd felt the drop in temperature too. Before he left we agreed to meet tomorrow at his place.

The Nimrods lived close to where we used to live, before we moved to End House. Going back there made me feel homesick. It all seemed so safe and normal and — well, unghostly. On Sunday afternoon Jay and I sat upstairs in the room he shared with his older brother Sam, talking in low voices.

"I never used to believe in ghosts," Jay said. "I thought it was just your imagination, Alex."

"So did I," I admitted. "In fact, the first time I saw him, down by Stackfield Pond, I called him the nightmare man."

Jay stared at me. "Why?"

"Remember that conversation we had, about what scared us most? I thought maybe I'd conjured him up, that he was my worst nightmare come to life. And that was even before I'd seen his face."

Jay asked, "Do you still have that dream you told me about?"

"Not since the night we moved into End House. But then I don't need to, do I? It's with me all the time."

We both fell silent. I couldn't shake off the feeling that it was me the Raven was haunting, not just the house — and that it was some kind of test to prove how easily I could be scared.

After a while Jay said, "Anyway, you couldn't have dreamed up the feathers. They were real enough."

"Yes," I agreed. "And it couldn't have been Harry Tate playing tricks, because I found the first feather before he overheard you and Emily and me talking in the loft, so he didn't even know about the Raven then."

Jay looked thoughtful. "I still think there's something odd about him."

I asked, "Have you ever heard of misdirection?" When he shook his head I explained what it was and told him what I'd found in the skip.

"But if it was just ordinary old clothes," Jay said, "why should he want to stop us looking inside?"

"I don't know. But the other day he said that people who try to scare you off usually have something to hide. So maybe there was something else in there that I missed."

Jay frowned. "Do you think that's why he put the stuffed raven outside your bedroom door, to scare you off?"

"It's possible. But to scare me off *what*?"

Jay didn't answer.

After a long pause he said, "How'd you like to stay

82

here tonight? We can take the mattress off my bed and put it on the floor."

"What about Sam? Won't he mind?"

"He won't have to." Jay grinned. "He owes me a favour, anyway. Let's go downstairs and ask mum now."

The thought of a night away from End House was tempting. A whole night without waking up and listening for noises — it seemed too good to miss. But wouldn't I be running away, trying to dodge the test?

"After all, I came to stay with you last weekend," Jay added. "So I reckon you owe me a visit."

That settled it. We went downstairs and asked Mrs Nimrod if I could stay the night. She said yes, provided my parents agreed. I said I'd go straight home and ask them.

"Well, I hope for Jay's parents' sakes you don't get up to the kind of tricks you both got up to last weekend," Mum said. "Otherwise I've no objection. Have you, Colin?"

Dad yawned and said no, he hadn't either. He was flaked out in the armchair again, just like last Sunday afternoon. Emily had gone out with Debbie Grover and Harry didn't seem to be anywhere.

"You'd better take clean pyjamas," Mum said. "You'll find some in the airing cupboard."

"Okay; thanks, Mum."

"And don't forget your toothbrush," Dad called after me.

I collected clean pyjamas and a toothbrush and shoved them into my flight bag. 'Flight', I thought, described exactly what I was doing — escaping from End House, if only for one night. Then I remembered I'd need a clean shirt for school tomorrow morning, so I shoved that in as well, together with a clean pair of socks.

I went downstairs again, but just as I was about to go back into the living room to say goodbye I heard something through the half-open door that stopped me in my tracks.

"Oddly enough," Dad was saying, "it looks as if there may be some connection with the Raven."

"The Raven?" Mum repeated.

"The method of gaining entry sounds suspiciously similar to that used by a confidence trickster who used to operate in London some years ago. He ended up doing time in the same jail as the Raven — in fact he was released a couple of months after old Cheyney died, which would tie in roughly with when this villain first appeared in the Bursley area."

They were talking about the man who went round tricking old people into letting him into their houses. I knew I shouldn't eavesdrop, but I also knew that if I walked in on this fascinating conversation Dad would stop at once. He always did. So I stayed outside the door and listened.

"But that's just one man," Mum was saying. "I thought you said there were several of them?"

"We now believe there's only one. Apparently the Crow is known to be fond of disguises."

"The Crow?"

"Otherwise known as Henry James Tatfield."

"But surely crow's just another name for raven?" Mum sounded puzzled. "I suppose they couldn't have been the same man, by any chance?"

"No, the Crow's much younger. And the Raven's quite definitely dead, there's no doubt about that. But it's possible the Crow may have modelled himself on the Raven, since the two men had a lot in common.

Quite apart from both being particularly crafty villains, they shared an interest in birds. In fact that's probably how they got to know each other."

"You mean they were friends?"

"Far from it. Perhaps they were too alike, in some ways. No, according to what I've been told they ended up deadly enemies."

Mum said, thoughtfully, "It does seem a strange coincidence. Do you know what the Crow looks like?"

"Not yet. We only contacted the Essex division yesterday. There's some information on Henry Tatfield winging its way to me right this minute — including, I hope, a photograph. By tomorrow we should have a better idea who we're looking for, even if he is a master of disguise."

It was those words, 'master of disguise', that gave me the clue. Upstairs, in the loft, was a wicker basket full of disguises — wigs, false moustaches, workmen's overalls — all belonging to a man who said he'd been out of work for the past few years, due to ill health.

Ill health — or doing time in prison?

Henry Tatfield — or Harry Tate, the man with something to hide?

Certain I was right, I opened my mouth, ready to burst in and tell Dad that the con man was right under his nose, living in the same house. But at that moment a hand clamped itself roughly over my mouth and I was dragged backwards, away from the door.

Seventeen

Prisoner

I struggled hard, but it was no use. Harry Tate was much stronger than he looked. He carried me upstairs as easily as if I were a baby, holding his hand over my mouth to stop my yells from being heard. When we reached the landing, he kicked the door to the attic staircase open with his foot. The lock gave easily. He shut it behind him and, at the top of the stairs, set me back on my feet.

"If you scream," he muttered in my ear, "I'll have to gag you."

As soon as he took his hand from my mouth I said, "You won't get away with this. Tomorrow Dad will know who you are."

He laughed softly. "Tomorrow's another day, young Alex. And that gives me one more night to find what I came for." Still with his arm clamped around my chest, he edged towards the skip.

"What's that?" I asked. "What was it you came for?"

"Don't you know? You're so darned clever I'd have thought you could work it out for yourself." With his free hand, he opened the skip and took out a length of rope. "I used to think Emily would be the problem here, but I was wrong. You may be the quiet one, Alex, but just lately you've been getting far too sharp for your own good."

He dragged me over to a chair and forced me to sit on it while he tied my wrists together. When I tried to resist he hit me hard across the face, swearing under his breath. The pain brought tears to my eyes. By the time I'd recovered he'd wound the rope several times around my chest, binding me to the chair. I thought about calling for help, but knew that Mum and Dad would never hear me. They were too far away. Besides, I didn't want to risk another blow.

"Remember this trick, Alex? When Emily tied me to the chair I escaped easily, didn't I? But these knots are different. I don't think it'll be so easy for you to get out of this." Taking another length of rope, he bent down to tie my ankles together.

I licked my lips, which had gone very dry. "I'm not afraid of you, Harry," I said — and to my surprise I realized I meant it. I was too angry to be afraid.

"Is that so?" His small mouth twitched, but not with amusement. "You're afraid of the ghost, though, aren't you? You're afraid of poor old Arthur."

I didn't want to think about the Raven. I asked, "Why did you call yourself the Crow?"

"Don't they teach you anything at that school of yours?" He nodded at the name painted on the side of the skip. "The Great Corvo. Corvo's Latin for crow — and not even your father got the connection. That's rich, that is."

Chuckling, he turned away to survey the heavy old

furniture belonging to the Raven. "It has to be here somewhere," he muttered. "There must be something I've overlooked." He started to wrench drawers out of the writing desk and put his hand inside the compartments, as if feeling for something.

"Stealing from old people's mean," I said. "You said yourself it's about the lowest thing anyone can do."

"Fools deserve everything they get," Harry said. "Most of 'em keep their savings under a mattress or in a piggy bank on the mantelpiece. That's asking for trouble."

He's heartless, I thought; no sympathy for anyone. The only living creatures he seems to care about are his pigeons.

With an exclamation of disgust, he left the writing desk and turned instead to the stuffed birds. He picked up the glass case containing a pheasant. "Now this," he muttered, half to himself, "is exactly the sort of hiding place the old buzzard would choose." Using a curtain to muffle the sound, he smashed the glass against the back of a chair, then took a penknife out of his pocket, snapped it open and started ripping the bird apart.

There was something cruel about it, even though the bird was stuffed. It sent a shiver down my spine. I said, "What are you looking for, anyway?"

"Shut up, Alex."

Suddenly everything was clear to me. "It's money, isn't it? You think the Raven left a load of money hidden somewhere in this house. That's why you came here — and why you wanted to put your gear into the attic, so that you'd have an excuse to search the place. No wonder you offered to sweep the chimney. You've even been digging in the garden!"

He tossed the remains of the pheasant aside and took up another glass case. "Cheyney was like all the other old fools — he couldn't resist boasting about his wealth. Nobody'd ever find it, he said — and he was putting a policeman in charge to make sure they didn't."

"You think that's why he left the house to Dad?"

"Seems like it."

It didn't sound a very likely explanation to me. All the same I was beginning to understand a lot more than I had before. "You won't find it," I said. "And even if you do, the Raven will make sure you don't get away with it."

"His ghost, you mean?" Harry laughed scornfully. He tossed the second bird aside, then glanced at his watch. "I suppose I'd better show up for tea, or it may arouse suspicion. Alex, I'm going to have to gag you."

"What's the point?" I tried to sound as reasonable as I could. "Even if I yell, no one will hear me."

"Sorry, old son. Can't take the risk." He pulled a scarf from the skip and forced it into my mouth, tying it tightly round the back of my head. "Now, stay there — and be good."

I didn't seem to have much choice.

As soon as he'd left the room I doubled my efforts to free myself, but the rope seemed to get tighter rather than looser, and I was afraid of tipping the chair over and falling on the floor. The gag was desperately uncomfortable. I felt as if I were going to choke on it.

I tried to keep calm and use my head. Sooner or later, I thought, someone was bound to realize I was missing.

But Mum and Dad thought I'd gone to stay with

Jay. They wouldn't start to worry until tomorrow evening at the earliest, when I didn't come home from school.

Jay would realize, though. He was expecting me back at his house straight away. When I didn't show up he'd surely start asking questions . . .

I waited for what seemed like hours. My stomach began to rumble and I had a terrible thirst. I couldn't look at my watch because my hands were tied behind my back, but I knew it must be getting late.

To make matters worse, there was a storm blowing up. I could hear distant rumbles of thunder and the wind made eerie moaning noises down the chimney. Much more of this, I thought, and I shall start imagining things. So far I hadn't seen the Raven's ghost again, but I had the strangest feeling that he wasn't far away. It seemed almost as if he was waiting for Harry to make a certain move.

When Harry eventually came back, he said, "Bad luck, old son, you missed a good tea — sausage, egg and chips. Then your wretched sister trapped me into a game of Scrabble. Took me ages to get away."

I tried to say something, but of course it came out scrambled because of the gag.

"What's that, Alex? 'Fraid I didn't quite catch what you said."

He was baiting me. Determined not to let him see how much I hated it, I kept quiet and glared at him.

"She cost me a lot of time. Now I'll have to work fast." He started breaking open another glass case, this time containing a magpie. "By the way, your friend Jay Nimrod rang. I answered the phone. He said he was expecting you to stay the night at his house, so I told him you'd changed your mind."

90

I tried not to show what a blow this was.

He searched the magpie and flung it on the floor. "Only two more birds to go . . ."

There was a sharp crack of thunder, but Harry didn't even look up. He must have nerves of steel, I thought. Helplessly, I wriggled on the chair but it was no use; I didn't have a hope of breaking free.

Eventually, he tossed aside the last stuffed bird, looking annoyed. "Cunning old buzzard," he muttered, under his breath. "I was certain I was on the right track there, but I've searched every flaming bird in this house . . ."

His voice trailed off. The answer seemed to hit him at the exact moment it also hit me. We stared at each other.

"Oh no, I haven't," he muttered. "There's one bird I still haven't searched — and that's the most likely hiding place of all . . ."

The raven!

Eighteen

The Third Time

Harry waited until we'd heard Mum and Dad come upstairs to bed. He gave them about twenty minutes to settle down, then removed my gag. "It's no use making a noise, Alex. I slipped a strong sedative into their night-time cocoa. Once their heads hit the pillow they'll go out like lights." He started to untie me.

The relief was enormous. I rubbed my wrists and ankles and moved my jaw about. "Are you letting me go?" I asked hopefully.

"Not exactly. I've a job for you to do."

"What sort of a job?"

"You'll find out. Come on, we're going downstairs."

I stood up. Just for a moment it crossed my mind that this was my chance to make a run for it . . .

But Harry seemed to read my thoughts. He gripped my arm and muttered, "I warn you, Alex, if you try any funny business it'll be the worse for your

Mum and Dad — to say nothing of Miss Nosey Parker Emily. You don't want to see them hurt, do you?"

I shook my head.

"Well, then — come on."

He kept hold of my arm as we went down the attic stairs, finding our way with the torch. When we reached the landing there was a flash of lightning, followed soon afterwards by a loud clap of thunder. If this doesn't wake Mum and Dad, I thought, nothing will. The temptation to call out was great, but I was afraid that Harry would only gag me again. At least I could now breathe freely and move my arms and legs. For the time being it seemed best to play along with whatever he wanted me to do.

That was until I realized what the job was that he had in mind.

He made me take the stepladder from the cupboard under the stairs and set it up in front of the front door. "Now climb up and switch off the burglar alarm," he ordered.

"I don't know how," I said, playing for time.

"Don't worry about that. Just get up there."

Slowly, I climbed the steps until I drew level with the raven's evil beak. Its beady yellow eyes looked straight into mine.

"You could have done this on the night you used the bird to play a trick on me," I pointed out.

"I didn't think of it then." He shone the torch on to the wall. "Found the switch? Right, now turn it off and pull out the wires."

I didn't want to touch the bird. I couldn't rid myself of the feeling that it was still a living thing, quite different from those other stuffed birds in the glass cases.

"What are you waiting for?" Harry growled. "Christmas?"

Gritting my teeth, I pulled out the wires.

"Good," said Harry. "Now, lift it off the wall."

I felt sick in my stomach. "Why aren't *you* doing this?" I demanded. "You didn't need to bring me downstairs. You could have managed quite well by yourself."

"I wanted the company. Get on with it."

I knew very well why he was reluctant to handle the bird himself. The last time he'd done it the Raven's ghost had appeared and he didn't want to risk it happening again. It didn't make me feel any better either.

"I'll pass it down to you," I muttered.

The bird was fixed to the wall in two places, by wire looped over a couple of hooks. It was difficult to reach them because of the outstretched wings. I detached first one piece of wire, under the tail, and then the other, which passed through its chest. As soon as I'd done that the whole weight of the bird rested on my hands. It was much heavier than I expected. It was also very cold.

Then I felt a little fluttering in its chest, like a heartbeat. I threw it down to Harry at once. Taking him by surprise, it nose-dived through his arms to crash on to the floor.

For a moment we were both transfixed, staring at the bird. As we watched its feathers seemed to lift slightly in a sudden draught of air. A shiver went down my spine, but then, from my vantage point on top of the stepladder, I saw what Harry couldn't see.

The draught was coming from the kitchen window. Someone had opened it and was climbing through . . .

It was Jay!

His telephone conversation with Harry must have made him suspicious and now he'd come to see what was really going on. Afraid that he might speak as soon as he saw me I said loudly, "Well, Harry? Aren't you going to search the raven?"

"Keep your voice down," he muttered.

"I thought you said Mum and Dad couldn't hear?"

He shot me an irritated look, but most of his attention was given to the bird lying on the floor. To my relief, I saw that Jay had got the message. He was standing by the kitchen door, just out of Harry's line of vision, signalling to me that he understood. If I hadn't switched off the burglar alarm, every bell in the house would be ringing by now . . .

"Come down from there," Harry snapped.

As soon as I reached the floor I saw what he wanted me to do. "Oh, no," I said. "You can do your own dirty work. I'm not touching that bird again. Besides," I added, "you'd have to trust me with the knife."

"I'd sooner do that than have to take my eye off you," Harry held out the penknife. "You couldn't do me much harm with this anyway, so I wouldn't try if I were you. Go on, get to work."

I was aware of Jay standing a few yards away, watching us from the shadows. Taking the knife I knelt by the bird. One eye looked up at me brightly. I could almost have sworn it blinked.

Its feathers moved again. This time the draught seemed to be coming from all around us and the cold was intense. My heart was thumping loudly in my chest. I felt Harry's knee in my back, giving me a nudge, and gripped the penknife tightly. But as I moved closer still the raven's wings flapped once, twice — and then there was a flash of blue lightning that lit up the entire hall. It seemed to strike the floor in front of me, right where the raven lay, and was immediately followed by a violent crash of thunder.

I jumped backwards, stumbling against Harry. He gave a muffled exclamation and pushed me away roughly. His eyes were fixed on the raven — and when I looked again I saw why. It was now standing upright, beating its wings.

"You old buzzard!" Harry yelled, his face red with fury. "You think you've beaten me again, don't you? But I'll get even with you, see if I don't."

As if in answer to his threat a circle of small flames sprang up around the raven, yet strangely enough there didn't seem to be any heat coming from them, only cold. I watched in stunned amazement as the flames grew higher and fiercer. Inside the circle of fire the raven too began to grow, rising upwards, changing its shape . . .

And that was when — for the third time in my life — I saw the nightmare man.

Nineteen

Escape

He stood in the centre of the flames, a man with the face of a bird. But as I watched he changed again, briefly showing me the face of an ordinary man, slightly balding (Arthur Cheyney — I felt sure of that!) before disappearing from sight behind the wall of fire that had sprung up between us. Now, suddenly, I could feel the heat. It was a real fire, hungry tongues of flame flickering across the carpet, cutting Harry and me off from the front door and trapping us against the wall. On the other side Jay had come out of the shadows and was staring at us, the flames reflected in the lenses of his glasses.

"Jay!" I shouted. "Get Dad. He's upstairs, sleeping."

He shook his head and began to back away. It was only then that I remembered his fear of fire. "You've got to warn them," I urged. "They've been drugged, they won't wake up unless you make them."

Jay hesitated. Already the flames were beginning

to take hold, spreading across the hall towards the stairs.

"Hurry!" I yelled. "While there's still time . . ."

Now I couldn't see him for smoke. The fumes were choking me, making my eyes sting and my throat rasping and raw. Blinded, I stumbled backwards and was immediately seized by Harry.

"Quick — through here!" Using the curtain to protect his head, he broke the narrow slit of a window just above my head, knocking out the single pane of glass. "You're small, Alex, you should just about be able to make it." He hoisted me up, pushing me over the sill.

It was a tight squeeze all right, but I managed to wriggle through, landing heavily on the ground outside.

Harry's face appeared in the opening. "Go and get help. Tell the neighbours to ring 999."

"But what about . . .?"

"Don't argue. Do as I say."

I fled next door and rang the doorbell frantically, throwing gravel up at the windows and shouting until somebody came. As soon as I'd made sure they understood I ran back to End House. By now all the downstairs windows were flaming and, from inside, came the sound of crashing timber. I tried to reach the front door but the heat drove me back.

Looking up, I saw pale, scared faces at the bedroom window . . . Mum's, Emily's, Jay's — I had to *do* something and do it quickly. Then I remembered the long ladder Dad had used when he was decorating the outside of the house. It was still lying in the back garden. I ran to fetch it, dragging it along the ground until I arrived below the window. It took all my strength to raise it until it reached to just below the windowsill. Then Dad reached out to steady it and I held firm to the bottom rungs.

Mum came down first, with Emily right behind her and then Jay. We all hugged each other and I said, "I was afraid you wouldn't wake up."

"It was Jay who saved us," Mum said. "He shook your father awake and then he went to fetch Emily. We owe him our lives." She hugged Jay as well, which made him look a bit embarrassed but also quite pleased.

Suddenly I realized Dad hadn't come down the ladder yet. I looked up and saw that he was still on the window ledge, staring down at us as if he couldn't move. Thinking he must be feeling the effects of the drug Harry had slipped into his cocoa, I started up the ladder towards him. But when I drew nearer I saw that the look in his eyes was fear . . .

Then I remembered that other time he'd been on a window ledge, ten years ago, struggling with the Raven, and had fallen twenty feet. "Dad," I said, urgently, "you must hurry. The fire's getting fiercer."

He stared at me for a moment, then seemed to recover his senses. Smoke was already billowing out of the window behind him. "Okay, Alex. I'm coming," he said, climbing on to the ladder.

When we reached the bottom there were more hugs all round. Suddenly I asked, "Where's Harry?"

We all looked round. There was no sign of him.

"He pushed me through the little window in the hall," I explained, "but he couldn't have got through himself. It was too small."

Dad said to Mum, "I'd better go back."

"No!" she protested. "Please, Colin . . ."

But he'd already gone.

Emily called after him, "Dad! Dad! Don't forget the pigeons."

"The pigeons will be all right," Mum said. "They're in the garden, well away from the fire. It's your father who's in danger."

Soon after that the fire engines arrived. Mum told the Chief Fire Officer about Dad going to look for Harry, and he said, "All right, Mrs Mackay, we'll get him out of there, don't worry."

Even so, it was some time before Dad staggered into view, covered in soot and with his eyebrows singed right off. "Couldn't find him," he gasped. "Looks like he's had it, poor devil."

By morning End House was just a blackened shell. In the first light of dawn Dad, Mum, Emily and I stood wrapped in coats lent to us by neighbours, surveying the ruin. Jay had been taken home by one of Dad's colleagues from the station, who'd turned up to help. Now only a few firemen were still around, picking over the charred wreckage.

"Everything lost," Dad muttered. "All our possessions, furniture, everything . . ."

"Not quite everything," Mum said. "We've still got our lives."

"Yes, we're the lucky ones." Dad gazed at the still-smoking ruin of End House. "They haven't found him, you know. Not even his body."

He looked grim. By now he knew that Harry was the Crow. I'd told him everything, including how the fire had started, although I don't think he altogether believed me.

"I expect he got away," Emily said. "After all, he was an esca — esca — what was that word, Alex?"

"Escapologist," I said.

"That's right. I expect he's used to escaping from burning buildings."

I hoped he had escaped. Okay, so Harry Tate was a villain. He'd robbed old people and kept me tied up for hours and generally been pretty rotten. But he'd also saved my life by pushing me through that window, so he couldn't have been all bad. I didn't like to think of him dying in the fire. Had the Raven really won, after all?

Dad said, "I'm proud of you, Alex. I'm proud of the way you kept your head when dealing with that villain. If you'd panicked it would have been the worse for you and for all of us. He was a dangerous man. You showed great courage."

He wandered off to talk to the firemen who were still sifting through the rubble, and Emily went with him. Of course I was pleased at what he'd said, but I couldn't help thinking that it had never been Harry who scared me, only the nightmare man.

I said to Mum, "Do you know what I think? I think the real reason why the Raven left End House to Dad was to cause trouble. He knew that if he told the Crow there was money hidden there he'd come to look for it, and that meant his two worst enemies would meet up with each other. It was probably his idea of a joke."

"Some joke!" Mum shuddered. "To be honest, I'm not sorry the house has burned down. I was never happy there. Now, perhaps, we can go back to living in a proper home again."

She got her wish. The ground where End House had stood was eventually cleared and a block of flats built in its place. But long before then we'd moved into a house not far from where we used to live, in the same

101

street as the Nimrods. Harry's pigeons came with us, and are now looked after by Emily. I'm always half-expecting Harry to come back for them one day, but so far he hasn't. The police haven't caught him either. I don't know if that means he's given up being a villain or has just got craftier.

Or if perhaps he didn't escape from End House after all, even though they never found his body.

As to whether the stuffed raven over the door actually contained Arthur Cheyney's secret horde of money, none of us will ever know. It was burnt to a cinder.

The strange thing is that I've never had that nightmare again, the one where I'm being chased by something I can't see, with flapping wings. Maybe it's because I've now seen that Dad too can be scared, so it doesn't seem as important any more.

Or maybe it's because, like Jay, I've now met my worst fear face to face — and overcome it.

Other books you will enjoy,
about real kids like you!